A Distinguished Thug Stole My Heart 2

Meesha

Lock Down Publications and Ca$h
Presents

A Distinguished Thug Stole My Heart 2
A Novel by *Meesha*

Meesha

Lock Down Publications
P.O. Box 870494
Mesquite, Tx 75187

Lock Down Publications
Like our page on Facebook: Lock Down Publica-
tions @
www.facebook.com/lockdownpublications.ldp
Cover design and layout by: **Dynasty Cover Me**
Book interior design by: **Shawn Walker**
Edited by: **Tisha Andrews**

Stay Connected with Us!

Text **LOCKDOWN** to 22828 to stay up-to-date with new releases, sneak peaks, contests and more…

Thank you!

Submission Guideline.

Submit the first three chapters of your completed manuscript to ldpsubmissions@gmail.com, subject line: Your book's title. The manuscript must be in a .doc file and sent as an attachment. Document should be in Times New Roman, double spaced and in size 12 font. Also, provide your synopsis and full contact information. If sending multiple submissions, they must each be in a separate email.

Have a story but no way to send it electronically? You can still submit to LDP/Ca$h Presents. Send in the first three chapters, written or typed, of your completed manuscript to:

LDP: Submissions Dept
Po Box 870494
Mesquite, Tx 75187

DO NOT send original manuscript. Must be a duplicate.

Provide your synopsis and a cover letter containing your full contact information.

Thanks for considering LDP and Ca$h Presents.

Dedication

Keep watching over me, Ladybug, you helped me through this one. I felt you all the way through those scenes. Lol. Continue to rest easy, baby!

This one goes out to my Breezy Baby! Thank u, babygirl for being there with your mommy through all the tough times that we endured throughout the years. Without you by my side, I don't know where I would be. It feels good to hear the words "I'm proud of you, Mommy". I love you, baby.

I released this book on January 8th because there are so many that have this birth date. So a birthday shout out goes to my Teetee Sherri! Happy Birthday, Geeb! I love u, baby. Monique, Happy Birthday, boo! If don't no one ride for me, I know you do! Love you, chic.
Happy birthday to Joshua and Ty'Asia.

Meesha

Chapter 1

Nova

This nut case was out of his mind if he thought Grant Davenport wasn't about to clap back on his ass. First, the stupid bitch that was never a friend of mine, hit me upside the head and stuffed me in a trunk. She had to get me while my back was turned because she knew I would've whooped that ass. But it's cool, her day is coming as soon as I get out of this place. Secondly, this delusional bastard went along with her simple ass plan, then had the nerve to act hard over the phone. Both of them just signed up for a one-way ticket to Oakwood— Cemetery, that is.

"You know you done fucked up, don't you?" I said, chuckling uncontrollably. Catching my breath from laughing so hard, I turned my head and spit against the wall. "You already know that you're gonna die don't you, Mr. Banks?" I looked this nigga in his eyes and didn't care what he would do to me. The expression on his face said it all. He was pissed.

"I'm not worried about that bitch ass nigga! And keep talking shit. I'm gon' swell yo' ass up, bitch!" he spat, while walking toward the bed that I was bound to. "You have been talking slick since you opened your eyes. I don't know where all this wanna be savage shit came from, but I can easily put yo' ass back in a hoe's place." His fist was balled up tight and he was shaking slightly.

I didn't give a fuck. If he was going to kill me, he needed to handle that shit. At this point, I wasn't scared to die.

I've survived my parents dying, this nigga stomping on my heart, breaking my fuckin' jaw, choking the fuck out of me and, finally, shooting me in my fuckin' head. Now his

9

goofy ass just added this shit to the list. What did I have to lose? Not a muthafuckin' thing! So, what happens shall happen.

"You think standing over me is supposed to scare me, Kelvin?" I turned my head waiting on him to respond, but he didn't say anything. He stood there looking down at me with his top lip curled, looking like a black ass Elvis reject. "That's what I thought. You know muthafuckin' well the bitch that you're looking at now isn't the same bitch that took all of that pussy shit you were dishing out before. You and that bitch is gonna see me when I get out of this bitch. You will be seeing your mama again real soon, nigga."

"Why are you standing there letting this bitch talk to you like that?" Ziva yelled.

"Bitch, I advise you to shut the fuck up, envious ass hoe!" I shot at her.

Ziva looked at Kelvin with her hand on her hip. "Kill this bitch before I do it for you! She's not gonna keep disrespecting me," she spat, walking towards me.

Kelvin turned and grabbed her by her arm, stopping her in her tracks. "You ain't about to do shit to her!" he said through gritted teeth. "Take yo' ass over there and wait!" he yelled, pointing toward the stairs.

"That bitch still got you playing Captain Savior and she's laying her ass there talking about your fucking mama! You soft for her ass, Kelvin! The love that you obviously still have for her is gonna get your ass killed! Get rid of this bitch and stop playing with her!" she yelled, while shaking her head. Ziva turned and walked in the direction that he pointed, not saying anything else. Kelvin kept his eyes trained on her with every step she took.

He turned back around facing me, then he lunged at me and grabbed me by my jaws firmly. He had a death grip on my shit. I guess that bitch words hit a nerve.

"Didn't I tell you to shut the fuck up? You want me to beat yo' ass, huh? You like that shit, don't you?"

He squeezed my jaws tighter and I never saw his other hand raise. Before I knew what was happening, he punched me in my face. My teeth entered my bottom lip deeply, drawing blood. I didn't know how my lip was freed, but I felt the small hole that was there. I ran my tongue over it repeatedly, but my mouth filled up rather quickly with the metallic tasting substance.

"You hit like a bitch, nigga," I laughed with blood running out of the corners of my mouth. "That's all you got? That punch was soft as hell, but you're trying to come at a boss like G. Yo' ass got a lot of practicing to do. That's not gonna do it." I gathered all the blood and saliva in my mouth and spit that shit in his face.

"Bitch, that's the worst thing you can do to a muthafucka!"

He wiped his face on his shirt and jumped on the bed. He started punching me in the face like he was beating a nigga. I felt my eyes swelling up instantly. He was punching me so hard my face became numb, but I didn't shed not a tear. I was all cried out at that point. He was swinging with all his might, but I didn't even feel that shit. Punk ass bitch wouldn't think to go heads up with a man, but he kept finding ways to fuck me up. The punches kept coming. Shit, I couldn't cover up if I wanted to, so I decided to piss him off some more.

"Yeah, just like that, but you're gonna have to follow through with the punch to get a good connection, ya feel me? Try it again. This time don't forget to follow through." I lifted my head so he would have a clean shot, but he never swung.

11

He eased off the bed with his fist still balled up, looking at me while walking backwards. Never taking his eyes off me, he looked scared as hell. I laughed evilly.

"You don't have to watch yo' back yet, Kelvin. Shid, I'm still attached to this raggedy ass bed. I can't go no damn where, but you will have to watch that muthafucka when I get loose. Believe that shit. As for you, bitch," I said, staring at Ziva with a smirk on my face. "As soon as I get my claws in yo' ass, I'm gonna make sure your death is nice and slow. You're gonna feel every minute of the shit I instantly formulated in my mind when yo' ass hit me with that bat. But, I have a machete with your name on it. I'm gonna cut your fuckin' head off and piss down your throat, you snake muthafucka. Just thinking about it is making my pussy wet, you dirty ass bitch."

I had morphed into someone else at that point. My mouth kept filling up with blood, but I didn't feel any pain. I just swallowed the blood and kept smiling. Seeing the fear that was etched on their faces made me feel good. It didn't matter what happened to me, but all that was going through my mind was they better kill me.

Kelvin backpaddled and grabbed Ziva by the arm, pushing her toward the stairs. Climbing the first step, he paused and looked over at me. I was staring just as hard back at him. With a smirk on my face, I blew his ass a kiss. He hurriedly took the steps two at a time before that kiss of death made it to his ass.

Neither one of them hoes knew what the fuck was going on and that's how I liked it. I'm still Nova, but with a new meaning. Mysterious with a little bit of brilliance and power running through my veins. But little did they know, they just turned a good girl bad in the worst way.

***

I could hear these two idiots arguing back and forth about little bitty ole me. I didn't know exactly what was being said, but I kept hearing my name. Kelvin did a number on my fuckin' face. I already knew he did because my face was tight, so I knew it was swollen. I could barely see out of my left eye and my right eye was totally shut.

I closed my eyes and prayed to God, asking him to please allow me to get out of this mess for the sake of my child. The very thought of me being pregnant brought tears to my bruised eyes, the salt burning them. I tried to stop, I couldn't. Not when G didn't even know that he was about to be a daddy. That was if I got out of there, but one thing I did know was these muthafuckas can never find out I was having a baby. Kelvin would kill me for sure off that alone.

I needed to figure out how I was going to get out of here. He must've turned my phone off because I knew Monica's ass had already tried to track my phone with that Find My Phone app. I started trying to twist my wrist every way possible, trying to loosen the damn tape. It wasn't going to last forever and I was going to get loose.

I heard the door open and someone walking down the stairs. Whoever it was made their way to the bed and sat down.

"Nova, I'm sorry that I wasn't at the hospital when you got shot. But to be honest, I wanted you to suffer. Everything that you've been through has only made you stronger. You never gave up, but I needed you to fall." That was Ziva's bitch ass talking to me like I couldn't hear her, so I laid there and let her believe just that.

"I have so much that I want to tell you. I know we will never be friends again, so ain't no better time than now to get this shit off my chest. I've fucked every nigga you have ever

13

been with. Shid, I even fucked yo' daddy a couple times. I know you want to know why and I'm gonna tell you. Whenever I came to spend the night at your house, he was always looking at me. So, I let him do more than look, starting our sophomore year of high school."

If I could have gotten up at that point, I would've slapped the shit out of her. I couldn't believe my daddy was fucking my supposed to be best friend! And this bitch been fuckin' behind me since I started fuckin'! Who does that? Where the hell was my mama, I was thinking until this broad interrupted my thoughts as I tuned back in to what she was saying.

"Your daddy was a great lover in and out of the bedroom and he kept my pockets laced. Shid, he even bought me my first car. But when he told me that we couldn't do what we were doing anymore, I was beyond mad. He said that your mama found out about us. I was trying to figure out how, but if he thought I was about to just let it end like that after four muthafuckin' years, he had another thing coming," she said, pausing for a good minute.

Four years! She was having sex with my daddy for four years? Where the hell was I? I had no clue. Not even a little bit of suspicion. I was fighting back tears so she would continue. I didn't even know if she was looking at me or not, but I couldn't believe this shit.

"Nova, I'm sorry. You're never gonna leave this bed until you're dead, so I'm gonna just say it. I killed yo' bitch ass daddy and your stupid ass mama! That nigga turned his back on me and thought that was gonna be it. Nah, that's not how shit goes. Yeah, they hit a car head on, but it wasn't the other driver's fault. I forced them into that lane. Luck was on my side. The driver was drunk and couldn't react quick enough. So yes, I paid his ass back for using me for all those years. And that's when I started hating you."

14

This was too much for me to handle. I couldn't hold it in anymore. I openly started crying.

"Why Ziva? I took care of you like you were my blood sister. You consoled me in that hospital when I had to identify my parents remains! So, that night you left Monica's house, you didn't go to the store? You went to kill my fuckin' parents? Bitch, you better kill me and I bet not ever get out of here. I'm killin' you, bitch! And that's on my mama!" I screamed at her until my throat ached. I fought hard trying to get the restraints off until my wrists burned, but they wouldn't budge. All I could do was cry, but the bitch wasn't done.

"I was fuckin' Kelvin before you even met him. I allowed him to fuck with you, but he went and fell in love with you which was not the agreement. Obviously, it wasn't sincere because we had been sleeping together the entire time." She laughed like she had one up on me, but I will get the last laugh when it's all said and done.

She stood up off the bed and ran her hands up and down my thighs. "I'm gonna lick that pussy that I've been wanting to taste since college. I've always wondered why the niggas went crazy over yo' ass. I'll find out soon. Until then, keep it warm for me, bitch," she said, turning to make her exit.

I heard her footsteps when she walked up the stairs and the door slammed shut behind her.

"I'm gonna kill that bitch and she's gonna beg me every step of the way," I said to myself with a face full of tears.

Meesha

Chapter 2

G

Nova was pissing me off. I told her not to be moving around freely because that fuck nigga Kelvin was out there on that bullshit. But *nooooo*, she wanted to go out anyway. She called when she was almost at Monica's, so I couldn't tell her to stay put. She knew I would've came home and took her. I was waiting for her to call to let me know that her hardheaded ass was there safely so I could get back to business.

"Yo, G. Where ya head at, my nigga? I called your name three times and you ain't answered yet."

Quan was looking upside my head with a mug on his face. Lil' nigga didn't scare no damn body. I can't take him seriously at all.

"Is that your mean face, nigga?" I said, bending over laughing. "Nah, for real, fam. What's up?" I was trying to keep a straight face, but that shit didn't work. I busted out laughing again. "Straighten ya' face up, man. What's up?" I got one last chuckle in.

"Ain't shit that damn funny, but like I was saying until I found out I was talking to myself, I finally got a hit on that grey Chrysler 300. It belongs to that nigga Kelvin and the address Tonio gave us is connected to him, as well. It definitely paid off when he followed that bitch Ziva." This fool started doing the *Milly Rock.* He was excited that he finally got something. We were coming up with a lot of blanks on this nigga and the frustration was setting in.

I looked at my watch for the fifty-eleventh time. "Why you keep lookin' at yo' watch? Do you have somewhere to be or something?" Quan glanced in my direction while he continued to type on the keyboard.

"No, I don't have anywhere to be. Nova called me over thirty minutes ago saying that she was on her way home from Monica's. She hasn't called me to let me know she made it," I said as I snatched my phone from my hip to call her. The phone rang until the voicemail picked up. I didn't hesitate to call back, getting the same results. At that point, I had a funny feeling in the pit of my stomach.

"Something's not right, Q. She never lets my calls go to voicemail. I have a funny feeling something is wrong."

I started pacing back and forth, calling her phone again. Getting more frustrated as time went by, I didn't want to jump to conclusions, but this was unlike her. My baby been through too much, so I can't let anything else happen to her. I tried calling her one more time with no luck.

I stood there with so many thoughts running through my mind, I finally decided to call Monica. I dialed her number and pulled a blunt from behind my ear and lit it. Taking a pull, Monica answered.

"Hey, bro. What's up? Did you make it home yet?" she asked excitedly.

"Nah, Monica, I'm not home. Is Nova still there?" I asked, blowing out smoke. In my mind, I was praying she said yes, but my silent prayer went unanswered.

"G, Nova left almost an hour ago. She said she was going to stop at Michaels to pick up a couple of things. She should've been home by now. What's going on?" Monica was concerned. I could hear it in her voice.

"I don't know what's going on to be honest. She was supposed to call when she made it home. I don't think she made it, Monica, but I'm gonna find out. Give me a minute and I'll call you back." I tried not to let the worry I was feeling reach my voice. I hit the blunt deeply to calm my nerves, but it didn't work. I needed a fucking drink. The pressure of not knowing where Nova was started to take a toll on me.

"Make sure you call me back, G. She's been through so much. I'm going to stay calm because I don't want to think negatively. She's ok, bro. She has to be." Monica was nervous. I could hear her tapping her fingernails against a hard surface.

"Monica, don't worry. I'm gonna call you back."

Ending the call with Monica, I dialed Nova's phone again. This time it was answered. I let out a sigh of relief, but it was short-lived.

"What up, G?" I looked at the phone to make sure I dialed the right number because I knew damn well shouldn't no nigga be answering her phone.

"Who the fuck is this and where is Nova?" I screamed into the phone. My adrenaline was rushing at a raging pace. I clutched my phone so tight in my hand, I thought I would crush it. Quan jumped up, ready to go. He then started turning equipment off at rapid speed.

"This is Kelvin, bitch ass nigga. I heard you've been looking for me, but since you couldn't find me, you took my mama from me. That was the wrong move to make, nigga, but I took our bitch back. An eye for an eye, my nigga. Now let the games begin, muthafucka."

This muthafucka got a death wish for real. His ass really didn't know what my hood credentials looked like. He fucked up because he should've asked somebody about me. I played about a lot of things, but the ones I loved wasn't one of them. When that nigga laughed in my ear like the shit was a joke and had the audacity to hang up on me, I threw my phone across the room. It didn't break from the looks of it, but I didn't care about that. The only thing I could think about was the wellbeing of Nova.

"What the fuck is up, G? Who was that on the phone, man?" Quan spat with enough venom to kill a muthafucka if his spit touched them.

"That nigga got Nova, Q! He bet not lay one muthafuckin' hand on her! *I* killed his bitch ass mammy. She didn't have shit to do with that!"

I was so mad, I had tears streaming down my face. I felt like my heart had been ripped out of chest. Guilt was setting in because I was supposed to protect her. I never intended to fall in love with this woman in a matter of months, but it happened. This moment just validated that shit.

"We gon' find her man, I promise you. That nigga is dead!" Q walked over and wrapped his arm over my shoulder.

"Fuck that shit! Round up the troops and get they ass over here now!" I screamed, knocking his arm off me with a force so strong he stumbled. "Operation Goon Squad is in full effect, muthafuckas." I said, retrieving my phone from the floor.

***

Every member of my squad showed up strapped with Scony leading the pack. These niggas been down with me from day one and I taught them everything they knew. Grooming them to be the goons that I needed, I had trained an army. This nigga didn't know what he had done, coming for me like I was some type of peon ass nigga. He just started his countdown, though, because his clock was ticking. The longer it took for me to find his ass, the worst his death was going to be.

I walked into the main room in the Dungeon and looked around. My niggas were ready to tear into some shit, but we had some soul searching to do. I was about to take this nigga whole muthafuckin' family away from his ass.

"Find out where the rest of this nigga's peoples are. I don't care who it is, find 'em! Pat, I'm gonna need you and J-Dubb to find out where his family's funeral is being held. His ass can't dodge that.

"Aye, G. There's no need to do that. Word on the street is that nigga cremated his mom and his brothers last week. A lot of people are mad because he did the shit and didn't let anyone pay their respects," J Dubb said, shaking his head.

"Well, hit the streets and see what else them muthafuckas saying. They mad at his ass! Capitalize on that shit! I want every rock overturned, looking for this nigga."

I walked to the office, grabbed the blunts that I rolled off the desk and walked back to the meeting. I hadn't smoked this much in a long time, but it's much needed right now. I passed the blunts around and got a rotation going in that bitch. This situation had me in beast mode and I swear all I was seeing at that point was red.

"Tonio, I'm gonna need you to get Monica on the line so she can tell you everything there is to know about that bitch Ziva. I have a feeling she got a lot to do with everything that's been going on."

"We can tell her when we get to her crib, cuz. I was gonna do that shit anyway because I don't trust that bitch. When Conte told the story of her lil' hating ass, I wanted to kill her. You don't do shit like that to your supposedly best friend!" Tonio was heated. He hated a lying ass female with a passion.

"Scony, I need you to do a solid for me, brah. Go check on all the spots and the businesses. Make sure everything is all good. Take the money to the spot and distribute out the food to whoever is running low. And go check on Lovely, my nigga. I haven't heard from her in a minute. I'm also gonna need you to break the news about Nova to Jade." Scony nodded his head, letting me know he was on it.

"Quan, do what you do and try to trace Nova's phone. I'm gonna get Ziva's number, as well, so you can track that one, too. Speaking of that nigga, Conte, see what his ass knows. We may get lucky with him again. Other than that, we keep hitting these streets to see what we come up with. Hit my line with any new information. Don't hesitate, my niggas. Every little bit counts. We out this bitch and watch ya' backs. Ain't no telling what this nigga got up his sleeve," I said and ended the meeting on that note.

Everybody dispersed out of the Dungeon except Scony, Quan, Tonio and myself. I knew they were hanging around to make sure I was good. I'm not, but I won't show that soft shit right now.

"Yo, G. What about that bitch, Avah?" Scony asked, looking at me. I hadn't forgotten about her ass. As a matter of fact, she had been hitting my line constantly for over a month. I just didn't answer her ass. There was no reason to. The next time she called she would be seeing me, but not for the reasons that she thinks.

"Oh, she will be seeing me real soon, my nigga. Real soon," I said, hitting the blunt while walking toward the door. I couldn't continue to stand around in this muthafucka. I needed to find my future. Scony and Tonio was on my heels, but I kept moving. The blunt started to do what I needed it to do, but that shit wasn't going to last long. My mind was on murder and I wasn't going to calm down until I saw blood.

"I'm about to head to the spots and take care of that business, then shoot over to Jade's crib. Hit my line if y'all here anything. I'll get up with y'all a lil later," Scony said, getting in his ride and peeling off.

Tonio stood there trying to figure out my next move. "We are gonna go to Monica's and drop this news on her, but I want to drive around to see what the streets are saying about this fuck nigga," I said, while getting a couple more puffs in.

"That's cool with me. We can take my whip. We have been chasing this nigga too long. It's time to silence this shit so we can go back to livin', my nigga."

"Yeah, this nigga dodge game is strong, but he's gonna slip and I am gonna be right there to handle his ass," I said, jumping in the passenger seat of his truck.

He peeled out and hit Halsted with a vengeance. We jumped on the expressway at 127th and made our way to the city. When we made it to the westside twenty minutes later, we pulled up on Madison and Pulaski and saw this cat named Dilla standing on the corner by the gas station. I rolled the window down when we stopped in front of him.

"What up, Dilla? Have you seen a nigga named Kels around this way?" I asked him, blazing up another blunt.

"Nah, I haven't seen that nigga in a minute. He's been ghost since his people got popped. But word is he fuckin' with a bad ass chocolate bitch. I think her name is Zell, Zay. Some shit like that," he said, looking around pulling his scully down.

"Well, if you see that nigga, I don't give a fuck what time it is, hit my line. I got ten racks for that nigga's head, so don't hesitate to call."

"Aw shit, I got you, fam," he said, rubbing his hands together. I motioned for Tonio to pull off and we were out of that bitch. I didn't give a fuck about shit. I told Tonio to head over to Christiana.

"Are you out of yo' fuckin' mind right now? We just lit that bitch up a couple weeks ago."

"Call me crazy! If I roll through and a nigga jump hard, that's what the fuck is about to happen again. Let's go." I didn't even look his way when I said the shit. I was tired of playing with this muthafucka.

When we pulled up, these niggas were still on the same shit, just standing around nickel and diming, not paying attention to shit. I saw a lil' nigga that was there the day we came through that muthafucka and laid Sergio's ass down. I reached in my waistband and checked my bitch. Putting it back, I told Tonio to pull over and I jumped out. He jumped out behind me. I had on a black Sylvan vest with a black long-sleeved thermal shirt, a pair of black jeans with black Tims. I pulled my black scully down and walked up to this nigga.

"Aye, let me get a fifty," I said to his ass. He looked down to go in his pocket and I pulled my bitch out and put it to his head. His body went rigid, he was stuck.

"Where is that nigga, Kels? Yo' ass bet not lie either because I'll leave yo' lil ass stankin' right here. This is what ya ass need to be prepared for when you want to play a grown man's game."

This nigga stood straight up and laughed at me. That pissed me off. "I'm not telling you shit, bitch! Yo' ass around here killin' mamas and shit. I hope he kill yo' bitch, nigga. Let her muthafuckin' death be on yo' conscious, pussy ass," he said with a snarl on his face.

Before I could talk myself out of it, I blasted that nigga and didn't think shit of it. The only thing I saw was his brain matter fly out of the other side of his head. I didn't even wait for his body to hit the pavement before I walked away. These niggas were going to learn that I wasn't the nigga to fuck with. When we got back to the whip, Tonio was laughing and shaking his head.

"Where are we going next, Terminator?" he asked, starting up the car.

"Let's go to Monica's. I saw blood, so I'm cool now," I said, sitting back.

Meesha

Chapter 3

Monica

G called me looking for Nova and I was worried out of my mind. I bit my nails down to nubs pacing back and forth, unable to sit down for more than five minutes. I kept looking at my phone to make sure I didn't miss his call back. I've tried my best not to cry, but to no avail. I really hoped he found her soon and she's okay.

My phone rang and I jumped off the couch, running to the counter to answer it. I pressed the talk button without looking to see who was calling.

"G, did you find her?" I asked in a panicky voice. Biting what was left of my nails, I waited for his response.

"This ain't G, ma. It's me, Antonio. Ummm, I'm about to come through. Is that all right?" A smile instantly formed on my lips. Antonio and I had been spending a lot of time together and I was really feeling him. I think I'm going to give him a chance, a for real chance without comparing anything to my past relationships.

"Yeah, that's fine. Have you talked to G, Tonio? I'm waiting on him to call me back with information about Nova." I walked to the kitchen, grabbed a glass and put it under the ice dispenser on the refrigerator.

"Yeah, I've talked to him. As a matter of fact, he's coming through with me," he said, clearing his throat.

"Is everything all right, Tonio? Please tell me what's going on. I need to know something about my best friend!" I slammed the glass down on the counter and snatched the bottle of tequila from the cabinet. Pouring a double shot, I downed it and poured another one.

"We are on our way, baby. I promise we will fill you in when we get there. I want you to calm down, Mo. I'm on my way," he said, hanging up.

Something wasn't right about his call. He wasn't trying to tell me anything over the phone. Nova is not okay and he didn't want to tell me. He had never come over to my house with G if Nova wasn't here, as well. I had to calm myself down. I threw back my second double shot of tequila and poured another one. After downing that shot as well, I felt a slight calm wash over me.

I went back to the living room with my phone in my hand. I looked down at my attire. I had on black leggings with an oversized top and house socks. I was decent. Shit, I was in the comfort of my own home. I went to the 'Book' and looked at the pictures that I had of me and the girls. I missed Nova and I just saw her a couple of hours ago. When my eyes landed on that bitch Ziva I got volcano hot. I wanted to stomp her ears in that day at the mall, but Nova beat me to it. We don't do that jumping shit, so I had to lay low. But I was going to see her ass again.

I laid my phone down and thought about the surprise Nova was planning for G. That was the best news we had heard in a long time. We were all so excited. Nova would be the first one to have a baby and now she's missing. The sound of the doorbell brought my thoughts to a halt. I didn't realize how long I had been sitting, looking through the pictures. I stood up to answer the door and fell back against the couch. It took me several attempts to get up, but I finally managed. I didn't think three shots would have me feeling this good, but I guess I could say six since they were doubles. Yeah, that would do it.

Staggering to the door, I looked through the peephole to see who was there. I had to be sure with that stupid nigga Kelvin still on the loose. After verifying who was on the other side, I unlocked the door and stepped to the side.

"Hey, Monica," G said, giving me a hug and kissing my cheek. "Damn, shorty. Did you spill the whole bottle of alcohol on yourself? You smell like a liquor factory," he said, backing up waving his hand in front of his face.

"Fuck you, G. It's not that bad!" I said, swinging on him laughing and stumbling a little bit.

"Shit, I had to step back so you wouldn't burn my bushy eyebrows off," G said, brushing his finger over his brow while grabbing my arm with his other hand to stop me from tipping over.

"Get yo' ass off my woman. Don't be talking shit to her," Antonio said, laughing while pulling me in for a hug. "Damn, baby. He wasn't lying. How much did you drink? Come on so you can sit down," he said with his face scrunched up.

He guided me into the living room and sat me down on the loveseat. My head instantly fell onto his shoulder. "I didn't drink too much. Just three double shots," I said lowly.

"Shit, only three doubles? That's more than enough. I can't dwell on that right now. Babe, G wants to talk to you about something. Hold ya' head up and listen." Antonio pushed my head up and I turned to look at G, but my head fell back again.

"Damn, G, she is fucked up. She ain't trying to hear what we're saying tonight. Maybe I will just tell her in the morning," Antonio said, while rubbing my back.

He was looking down at me when I jumped up and ran to the bathroom and damn near put my head in the toilet. My mouth was watery and I kept spitting, but I knew I had to throw up. All I could do was spit and gag, spit and gag, in that

29

order. I heard someone walk up behind me and I knew it was Tonio.

Bending down next to me, he handed me a bottle of ice cold water. "Drink this, baby. It will make you feel better."

I took a couple of swallows of the water and immediately sat it down. Tonio grabbed my hair to keep it out of the toilet. That damn water forced me to throw up and everything came out like a faucet.

"Damn, baby! Ewwwwww, damn. What the—" Tonio started to say, gagging himself, but he never left my side. I was throwing up so much, I thought my organs were going to follow all the liquor that I was getting rid of.

Once everything came out, all I could do was dry heave. My rib cage was hurting like no other and it was painful to breathe. Tonio tried to get me to drink more water, but I wasn't having it. He left out of the bathroom and I struggled to get up. I rinsed my mouth and brushed my teeth. My head was pounding.

"Here, I'm gonna need you to take this, baby. It will make you feel a lot better," he said, handing me a packet of BC powder and the bottled water. I don't know where the hell he got it from because I had never had that shit. It was the nastiest shit I've ever tasted, but I took it like a champ.

"Let's go back in there. We need to talk to you," he said, wrapping his arm around my shoulder and leading me down the hall.

When we got back to the living room, G was sitting with his head in his hands. He looked up when we entered the room. I sat back on the loveseat and held my head down.

"I'm sorry about that. I've been worried sick about Nova and had a little too much to drink. But what's going on and don't lie to me. Did y'all find her?" I asked, looking up at G.

I was struggling to keep my head up, but I was determined to hear them out.

"No, we haven't found her, Monica, but I know who has her. Kelvin has her, but we are gonna get her back. You have my word," he said slowly.

The tears started flowing like Niagara Falls. I couldn't stop them no matter how hard I tried. Taking a breath, I tried to speak but failed miserably. After a while, I calmed myself down.

"G, Kelvin is crazy about her. If she doesn't do what he says, he will kill her. He doesn't want her to be with anyone but him. You saw how they came through shooting up her house! He didn't care if one of those bullets hit her or not. He was pissed because you were there with her." I sniffed.

"I will always be there with her! His ass better get used to that shit because I'm not going nowhere!" He calmed himself down and continued what he was saying. "He answered her phone when I called. He's mad because I killed his mama, so now he has Nova. I didn't know he would go after her, I swear. I'm sorry. I was supposed to protect her and I didn't." He broke down and cried like a baby. I had never seen a man openly cry like that in my life. At that point, I knew that this man loved my friend.

I stood up and walked over to him. "It's not your fault. Kelvin was going to find a way to get to her regardless once he found out she was still alive. He's just trying to make it seem like this is all on you. It's not. I don't blame you at all. You have been everything to my sister. And I appreciate you being there with her through everything, but I have something to tell you," I said, looking away and wiping tears from my eyes.

"She was so excited about telling you—" I couldn't continue because I was choked up. "She—she, came over to my

31

house because she was scared to do it alone," I cried out and sat down.

"Take your time, baby. What are you trying to tell us?" Tonio asked, hugging me tightly.

"She's pregnant, G. Nova is having a baby. She didn't want to take the tests alone. All five of them came back positive. You're going to be a daddy." I tried to smile, but the tears kept falling.

G looked at me with a shocked expression on his face. "She's pregnant with my baby?" he whispered.

"She found out earlier. She left my house and said that she was going to Michaels to buy a couple of things to make. She was going to set up a scavenger hunt to tell you about the baby," I said, looking at his tear stained face.

"Damn, cuz. We gotta find her, man. We can't let that nigga hold on to her too long," Tonio said, looking at G. "Baby, I'm gonna need you to give me any and everything you have on Ziva. I think she may have something to do with this. We are covering all angles," Tonio said, turning to look at me.

"Oh, I know everything about her trifling ass, but promise me if y'all catch up to her hoe ass, y'all will bring her to me first. I have a nice ass kickin' reserved just for her."

"Nah, you are too beautiful to be fighting, Mo. We will take care of it." Tonio was trying hard not to laugh.

I stood there for a moment, then it came to me. Ziva surely could've had something to do with this. "Y'all might be onto something. A couple of weeks ago, Nova beat the hell out of Ziva in the Woodfield Mall's parking lot. There was this dark-skinned chick that had a long straight weave with her. So yeah, she could still be mad about that," I said, getting mad all over again.

"Nova never told me about that!" G said angrily.

"Maybe she didn't want you to get mad at her, but she earned that ass whoopin'! I wouldn't have stopped it for all the money in the world," I said seriously.

"G, she just described that bitch Avah! You gotta pay that bitch a visit. She probably knows what the fuck is going on, too. We ain't playing with these hoes, man. They want to be grimey like niggas. We are gonna treat they ass just like them," Tonio yelled.

"Yeah, I'm on it, my nigga. That bitch knows something. She's pissed because I stopped fucking with her ass. But she's barking up the wrong muthfuckin' tree right about now. What Michaels did she go to, Monica?" he asked, standing up heading to the door.

"She went to the one in Chicago Ridge," I told him, putting on my shoes.

"Where do you think you're going, Monica?" Tonio asked, looking at me with one eyebrow raised.

"I'm going to look for my friend with y'all! What you thought?" I said, snapping my neck around to look at his ass.

"Nah, baby. That's not gonna happen. I want you to stay here and wait for my call. I'll be back tonight. I don't want you out there in these streets, baby. So just sit tight and get you some sleep. I'll be back," he said, kissing me on the lips.

"Make sure you call me, Tonio. I want to know if anything changes." I knew not to argue with him right then because he was pissed. Instead, I walked to the kitchen and gave him the spare key. "I may be asleep when you return. Let yourself in," I said, walking to my bedroom. I heard the front door open and close, then I crawled in the bed and cried myself to sleep.

Meesha

Chapter 4

Scony

I let G and Tonio head on over to Monica's house and I went to deliver the news to Jade. When I got there, she was cooking and dancing around the kitchen. The house smelled just like my grandma's on Sunday. I hated to come over being the bearer of bad news, but she needed to know. Nova is like a sister to her and I knew keeping this from her would put me in a bad spot.

"What are you cooking over there, sexy?" I asked, sitting at the table, removing my jacket.

"I made some cabbage with turkey meat, sweet potatoes, mac and cheese and cornbread. And a German chocolate cake for dessert," she said, looking at me with low eyes.

This woman was sexy as hell and she knew how to cook. I don't know about any other man, but that was the key to my heart. She was looking good as fuck, standing there in those booty shorts with a tank top on. My dick bricked up instantly, but that's not what I came over here for. I stared at her for a minute, not wanting to take that smile off her face, but I had to tell her.

"Come sit down for a minute, Jade. I need to talk to you," I said, playing with the salt and pepper shakers.

She sat down in front of me and grabbed my hand. "What's going on, Demarius? Is everything all right?" she asked with concern written over her face. I gave her a pass for calling me by my government. This wasn't the time to correct it.

"I don't know how to tell you this and I don't want you to be alarmed, but Nova is missing. She never made it home after leaving you and Monica earlier."

Jade let go of my hand and jumped up, frantically looking around. She was basically turning around in circles. "What are you looking for, Jade?" I asked, following her movements.

"I'm looking for my phone! I have to call Mo. She has to know about this. I wouldn't dare not tell her! We are all Nova has!" she yelled.

I got up and cradled her in my arms and the well broke. She was crying so hard, her body had a strong quake to it. I walked backwards until I got to the chair I was sitting in. I sat her in my lap and kissed her tear-stained face until she calmed down.

"You don't have to call Monica. Tonio and G is with her right now. I came to tell you myself, but there's more. Kelvin has her—" I attempted to tell her, but was cut short.

"Oh my God, Scony! He's gonna kill her! That man is crazy. He's one of those 'if I can't have you, no one will' type muthafuckas. She's not safe with him! We must find her, Scony. She's pregnant! We just found out today. She's fuckin' pregnant and that asshole has her!" She started crying all over again.

I was trying to console her the best I could when my phone started ringing. I shifted her body a little bit so I could reach in my pocket. I finally got my phone out and looked at the screen. G was calling.

"What up, brah?

"How is Jade? Let her know everything will be okay. I'm gonna find my baby, man." G didn't sound like himself at all. The last time I heard his voice like that was when his grandmother passed away.

"She's okay, G. This is tearing her up, man." I was rubbing her back as I was talking on the phone. She had settled down pretty much to a slight sniffle. "I don't want her here by herself, man. That nigga knows where she lives. I'm gonna bring her to Monica's."

She looked at me and nodded her head. She got up and went into the kitchen, taking Tupperware bowls out of the cabinets and started packing up the food.

"We are gonna wait here until you get here. We're about to go to Chicago Ridge. Nova went to the Michaels over there. I already got Q on his way. We're gonna go get the surveillance footage."

"G, they ain't giving us that footage, man. We ain't the police," I said, standing up and patting my pockets looking for a blunt with no such luck.

"When the fuck has that shit ever stopped us from doing anything? It's either they are gonna give that shit up or somebody ain't going home tonight, my nigga. They don't have a muthafuckin' choice in the matter. Now, we are waiting on you. The store closes in two hours. Make ya way." He hung up without giving me a chance to say anything else.

"Baby, are you ready?" I called out to Jade. She had finished packing up the food and went into the bedroom. I walked back to see what she was doing and she was putting on her shoes. She had an overnight bag, as well.

"Yes, I'm ready. Let me grab my phone, then we can go." She gathered her things and walked out of the bedroom. I grabbed the bags of food and her overnight bag, then we walked out the door.

***

The ride to Monica's was so quiet, I could hear myself thinking. I wanted to find that muthafucka and peel his shit

37

back. He had fucked with too many people's lives in a matter of months. It was time for him to take his last breath. Not only did he and his weak ass friends kill my cousin, now he wanted to add kidnapping to his shit, as well. I got a bullet that I'm gonna embed between his eyes and that's on Malikhi.

When we pulled up, Tonio and G was outside doing what I so badly needed to do. That was puff, puff, pass. I parked the car and got out. Walking to the passenger side, I opened the door and helped Jade out. I grabbed all the bags and walked them to the house. Tonio walked up and unlocked the door, letting us in. I wanted to say something about this nigga having a key, but I'll wait until I come back out.

I put the bags on the kitchen table and grabbed Jade around the waist. "I'll be back to get you. Go in there with Monica and be safe. If anything, and I do mean if anything happens, call me." I lifted her head up by her chin and kissed her deeply. I pecked her lips once more and headed for the door. "Lock up, baby. I'll be back." Walking out the door, I stood there until I heard the locks click in place.

When I walked up to my niggas, G handed me a much needed blunt. I didn't hesitate to blaze that bitch up. I took a couple of tokes and my mind stopped racing for a bit. I was thinking of all kinds of ways to kill this nigga when I got my hands on him.

"Let's roll out. Quan is gonna meet us at the store," Tonio said, popping the locks on his 2017 Mercedes GLC truck. Before any of us could move towards his ride, the door to Monica's house opened and both of the ladies came rushing out.

"What's wrong with y'all?" I asked, hitting the blunt and passing it to Tonio.

"I don't know why I didn't think about this before. We can locate Nova's phone on the Find My Phone app. We all have iPhones, so we follow each other to locate each other at any given time," Monica said, while accessing the app.

"Damn, her phone is not showing up. It says that it's offline. That can mean one of two things, her phone was turned off or it died. But I will keep checking it, though. I'm sorry, y'all. I thought I had something," she said, crying again.

Tonio walked over to her and hugged her. "You do have something, sweetheart. It just didn't help us at this moment. That nigga is gonna fuck around and turn that phone back on sooner than later. If you see something change, call one of us and let us know ASAP. But for now, I want y'all to go inside because we have moves to make." He leaned down and pecked her on the lips.

I turned to walk to the truck and called out to Monica. "Do Ziva have that app connected to her phone, as well?" I asked, turning in her direction.

"Yeah, hold on. Let me check to see if her location comes up." Monica searched her phone for a few moments and looked up, shaking her head. "Her phone isn't showing up either, but I will continue to check both."

"Okay, if you get anything from those phones, you call one of us ASAP," I repeated.

We all hopped in Tonio's truck and watched them go inside and pulled off. G's phone rang a few minutes later. It was Quan wondering where we were. He put the phone on speaker.

"Yo', where are y'all? I'm standing next to shorty's car right now. The doors were unlocked and the keys are on the front seat. This shit don't look good, brah."

"We are on our way now. Is the store crowded, fam?" I asked, trying to see how we were going to approach the situation.

"Nah, there's a few people inside, but I really don't know the head count. Do you want me to go in and find out?"

"Nah, we'll be there in about fifteen minutes, so just hold on. We will go in together. One," G replied, ending the call.

As we were driving, I figured this would be a good time to question Tonio's ass. "Fam, you got a key already, huh? You must've fucked her really good to have full access," I laughed and waited on his response.

"Mind ya' business, Scony. I haven't even had a chance to sample the pussy, but I want to make sure she's safe. I'm going back to her crib when we're done checking shit out." Tonio was serious as fuck right now. I understood where he was coming from, so I let it go. This was not the time to try to lighten the mood. Everybody's mind was on one thing and that was getting Nova back safely.

"I had to slump a nigga when we left you earlier. The nigga was talking reckless with a tool to his head. I silenced that muthafucka where he stood. These niggas are gonna stop testing me. Play time is over. There will be more blooodshed before it's all said and done," G said from the front seat.

I was kind of pissed that I missed out on a kill, but I will get a chance to make my bitch cum soon enough.

We pulled up and exited the truck. Q was standing by the door. We all walked into the store together and I spotted who I assumed was the manager on duty. "I'll take care of this one. This shit is gonna be easy," I said to G. He nodded his head and folded his arms with a smirk on his face. She was a thick chic and cute as hell. I walked up to her and sparked up a conversation.

"Hello, Miss Tiffany," I said, reading her name tag. "How are you? Are you the manager of this store?" I asked with a smile.

"Yes, I am. How may I help you?" She was looking back and forth from me to my niggas like we were about to rob the store. Shid, I was trying to be good, but her body was bangin'.

I was saying to myself, *Jade who?* But I had to check that shit and concentrate on the task at hand.

"Come walk with me, cutie." I motioned for her to walk down an aisle with me. She kept looking back to see what the others were doing.

"You ain't got nothing to worry about, sweetie. We ain't about to rob your store at all, but I do need something from you, though."

"What do you need from me?" She stopped walking and put her hand on her hip, smacking her lips. The professionalism was gone and Shaniqua showed up in full effect. All my thoughts dissipated right then. I hated a ghetto bitch. All she could do now was suck my dick. It wouldn't go any further.

"I need the surveillance footage from about four o'clock today to about seven. Nah, scratch that. I need the tapes from today period, including right now." I stood there rubbing my hands together, waiting on her response.

"I'm not losing my job for giving you shit that I'm not supposed to. You got me all fucked up. I got kids to worry about, so that would be a no from me," she said, turning to walk away.

I pulled a knot of cash out of my pocket and started counting out hundreds. That bitch knew the sound of money because her head whipped around like that little girl on *The Exorcist.* I was dying inside because she was just another female that would do anything for a dollar, but all I wanted was the fuckin' tapes.

"How does five hunnid sound, shorty?" I said, holding out the money.

"I'm about to risk my damn job and you talking about five hundred dollars? You can move round with that shit," she said, eyeing the money in my hand. I counted off another five hundred and you could see her mouth watering like a bottle of ice cold soda on a hot day.

"Is that enough for your ass, shorty? If not, I'll stuff my muthafuckin' Nina down your throat. Then you'll be doing the shit for free, with a jacked-up grill to match. Now make your choice and choose wisely."

She looked at me and reached for the money. I snatched it back and looked at her hard. "You ain't getting shit until you give me what I asked you for. We gon' do this shit at the same time. I don't know yo' ass like that. And keep this shit between the two of us. Don't make me come back to this bitch, because if I do, it's gonna be some slow singin' and flower bringin' for yo' ass. Do you understand what I'm saying?" I stared her in her face without blinking. She nodded her head up and down rapidly.

"Wait right here. I'll go make a copy for you," she said, backing up.

"Shorty, don't try no funny shit. I don't have no problem shooting yo' ass," I said through gritted teeth.

"I won't, I promise. I'll be right back." She damn near ran to the office to get the tapes.

I walked back over to where my niggas were and they just looked at me. "What the hell you say to that girl, Scony?" Tonio asked.

"I ain't said shit to her ass. Her money hungry ass had to understand that she wasn't playing with one of these lame ass niggas. I'm that nigga that ain't gonna play with her smart mouth ass. I shut her up, that's what I said to her," I said, grilling his ass.

They started laughing hard and shaking their heads. "You wild, nigga. You better stop doing that shit to these females, man," Quan said, walking outside. All he wanted was the footage so he could start working on finding out where the hell Nova was being held.

"Here you go. I was able to copy the entire footage for you. Now, can I have my money?" she asked, holding out the disc.

"Hell nah! Bring yo' stupid ass outside. All these damn cameras around here and you wanna be seen handing me some shit and my dumb ass paying you for it."

I turned and walked away from her and out the fuckin' door. She followed and got in the car with me and the exchange was made. She was about to get out of the car and I stopped her ass.

"Where the fuck you think you're going? I'm not finish with yo' ass! You must think I'm a dumb muthafucka. Give me your muthafuckin' ID, shorty."

She looked like she was against it, but thought better of it and took the ID card out of her back pocket. I took a picture of it with my phone and handed it back to her.

"Security. Now get yo' ass out and thanks." I placed the disc in my pocket, got out the car and walked to Q's ride. I reached in my pocket and handed him the disc.

"Hit us up and let one of us know what you come up with, Q," G said, walking over to Nova's car.

"A'ight, bet. I'm out. I'm getting on this tonight. Too much time has passed. We don't wanna sleep on this, nigga," Q said, getting into his car.

Meesha

Chapter 5

G

I walked over to Nova's car and opened the door. I picked up the keys and put them in the ignition to start it up. It cranked right up, so what the fuck happened? I looked around the car and noticed the bags in the back seat. I grabbed one bag and there were pink and blue confetti-like papers in little containers. I grabbed another bag and there were envelopes with little cards in them. The last bag had pink, green, yellow and blue markers in it. The tears started falling because this was a reminder that My Future was having my baby.

I grabbed her purse and lifted the plastic bag out and opened it. Inside were five pregnancy tests just like Monica said and they all had positive results. I laid the bag in my lap and my head fell onto the steering wheel. I started bawling like a baby. This situation with Nova had me emotional as hell. It's been so long since I've loved someone like this. I knew then that love had no time limits. I hadn't known her long, but I knew I loved her with every fiber of my being.

I wiped my eyes and got out of the car. I approached Scony and Tonio and said, "I need some time to myself. I'm calling it a night. I have nothing to go on right now and it's killing me. Y'all know I'm killing that nigga, right? Get the lawyers on speed dial because I don't give a fuck where I see that nigga at, I'm blowing his muthafuckin' brains out!" I said through clenched teeth.

"G, we will be right there with you filling that nigga with lead. We are riding this shit out together 'til the end. Ain't no

solo missions happening around these parts." Scony was looking in my eyes and I knew he meant every word that left his
mouth.

"Cuz, are you gonna be a'ight? Do I need to roll with you,
man? I can call Monica and tell her that I'll be by later. You're
my family and I want to make sure you're good." Tonio
wasn't trying to let me go off alone, but he wasn't coming with
me. I needed this time alone.

"Nah, Tonio. Go with ya girl. I'm about to go see Mom
Dukes. I'm straight. I'll catch up with y'all later." I dapped
them up and jumped in Nova's car and headed south to my
mom's. Nova's radio was playing every damn love song there
was in the industry. I turned the radio off and just drove in
silence. I didn't get an ill feeling, so I knew she was okay. I
missed her touch. Shit, I missed everything about her ass. I
pulled up to my mom's house and sat there for a few minutes
before getting out. I walked up the steps to the door and it
opened.

"Grant, what's wrong, baby?" she asked, hugging me
tightly.

I broke down right there in her arms. I didn't have to try
to hide the hurt that I felt. I didn't have to appear hard. Nah,
not with my mama. She let me go and closed and locked the
door. Leading me to the kitchen, I sat at the table and she went
straight to the cabinet and poured me a double shot of Henny
and brought me some weed and a blunt. Yeah, my mama already knew. She never judged. She was calm and understood.

"Now, talk to me, Grant. I already see that you're in street
mode and I'm all right with that, but I need to know what's
going on just in case a muthafucka try to come after me. I'm
not worried about it one bit, but don't leave me in the dark,
baby," she said softly, taking a seat.

My mom was forty-eight years old and didn't look a day over thirty. Her name is Clarissa Davenport, but everyone calls her Rissa. She had me when she was nineteen and did a fine job raising me into the man I am today. She did everything possible to keep me out the streets, but I found my way in them anyway. There wasn't a daddy around for me to look up to. It was only my moms, granny and me. I felt I had to be the man in the household. I didn't want my mom to have to work like slave to make ends meet. That is the reason I started working the corners and eventually taking over an entire empire.

"Ma, remember the woman I was telling you about?" I took a sip of the Henny and started rolling the much needed blunt. My mom already knew who I was talking about because I didn't talk about the other hoes I gave the dick to. There wasn't a point in doing so. Their ass never made it to Mom Dukes' door.

"Yes, Miss Nova. How is she? She didn't dump your high yella ass already, did she?"

"Nah, Mama. She was kidnapped by her ex and I don't know where she is. The nigga answered her phone talking real muthafuckin' tough. He took her because of something I did. It's my fault, Mama. I wasn't there to keep her safe." Tears welled up in my eyes and I felt like a bitch at that moment.

"What did you do to make him come for you, Grant?" she asked with her chin resting on her fist.

I held my head down for a minute and lifted it back up. I wasn't about to lie to my mama. I've always been straight up with her. "I killed his muthafuckin' mama and both of his brothers after his pussy ass shot Nova in her fuckin' head! That muthafucka went into hiding and to get him to come out, I took something close to his ass! I don't regret that shit either, Ma, but I feel bad because Nova didn't do it!" I stood up and

47

started pacing back and forth, trying to calm myself down. I lit the blunt and hit that shit long and hard, blowing the smoke out through my nose.

"Got damn, G. What did his mama have to do with that? You should've just waited until you caught up with him!"

"You're right, but what's done is done, Mama. I can't take that shit back if I wanted to. All I ask of you is to be careful and watch your surroundings. Keep that gun I bought you on you at all times and don't hesitate to shoot a muthafucka." I finished the blunt, walked over to the sink, put it out and tossed it in the trash. Sitting back at the table, I placed my forehead on the table and closed my eyes.

"I just found out that she's pregnant, Ma. My Future is having my baby and I don't even know where to begin looking to get her back. I want to be happy about the baby, but I'm more scared than anything now," I said with tears running down my face.

"It's going to be all right, baby. I know you love this girl. She has an angel watching over her. She has gone through a lot in a short amount of time and she has been strong enough to overcome all of it. You will find her, baby. It's just going to take time."

I heard what my mom said, but I wasn't feeling very confident about finding her safely. After a while, I raised my head and looked up at my mom. With bloodshot eyes, I reached across the table, running my fingers across her knuckles.

"Mom Dukes, would you please pray for Nova and my baby's safety? And pray for me as well, because I'm gonna need it. I'm killin' that nigga on sight and there ain't shit nobody can do to talk me out of it." I bowed my head, waiting on her to pray over her only son.

Once she finished praying, I didn't feel any better, but I was glad that I told my mama everything that was going on. I kissed her on her cheek and told her I was going home to get some sleep. I explained to her how important it was for her to be on alert and that I will be calling more than I had been. I left out of my mom's house and jumped right in the car and headed home.

Cruising on the expressway, my phone started ringing. I looked at the phone briefly and looked back up at the road ahead. I snubbed the call because it was that bitch Avah. I didn't have shit to say to her ass. I was going to kill that bitch, too, but I'm too tired for that shit right now. It was going to be easy as fuck to get to her stupid ass. Her day was surely coming.

I made it to my crib in like thirty -five minutes. I parked Nova's car in the garage next to mine. Making sure the garage door was completely down, I entered the kitchen and Lady came running right towards me and stopped. She looked around me and started whining. She was used to Nova being here. I may as well admit that Lady is no longer *my* dog.

"What's happening, Lady Love? Come on so I can let you out to take care of ya business."

I walked towards the patio door, but I didn't hear her behind me. I turned around and Lady was still in the same spot.

"Lady, come on, girl," I said, snapping my fingers. She still didn't move. All she did was lay down and whined. Damn, my dog was hurting just like I was. I finally got Lady to go outside, but she just took care of her business and came right back in. She went right back to the same spot in the kitchen to lay down.

I went into my bedroom and left the door open just in case Lady decided to come in. As I was removing my clothes, my phone rang. Looking at the screen, it was Avah again. I decided I would return her call tomorrow. Right now, I just wanted to lay down and get some sleep. I took a shower and

49

climbed into bed. I wasn't even used to sleeping alone anymore. Turning off the light, I turned over and closed my eyes.
Five minutes later, Lady jumped in the bed and curled up on
Nova's side. I didn't even bitch at her. I just closed my eyes
and fell asleep.

***

I woke up the next morning with Lady licking me all over
my face. I turned over and pulled the cover over my head and
she started nudging me in my back. I let her beat the hell out
of me for about ten minutes. Finally yanking the covers back,
I stared at her with the meanest look.

"Lady! What the hell is wrong with you? Can't you see
I'm trying to sleep? It's too fuckin' early for this shit!"

I was screaming at a damn dog as if she could scream
back. This bullshit with Nova had me on edge. Lady looked at
me with her puppy dog eyes and nudged Nova's pillow towards me. The scent of coconut oil could be smelled a mile
away. That made me miss her even more. I grabbed the pillow
and brought it to my face and the tears started flowing rapidly.
It must be true what people say about dogs knowing your feelings. I felt Lady lay her head on my chest and I started rubbing
her head.

"I'm gonna find her, baby, and I'm gonna bring her back
home. I promise," I sniffed, while rubbing Lady's head.

We laid like that for about twenty minutes when Lady
jumped up barking. I knew that she needed to go outside and
relieve herself. I threw off the covers and sat on the side of the
bed, finally finding the strength to get up. I slipped on my slip-
pers and grabbed my robe. Walking toward the door, I doubled
back. I needed to hit some of that good shit to get my mind
under control. I grabbed a sack of weed and a Swisher along
with my phone.

I exited my bedroom and when I walked into the living room, Lady was standing at the patio door doing the little doggy dance. I started laughing hard because I had never seen a dog dancing around because they had to piss. Nova turned my dog into a real bitch. I let her out and went to sit on the stool at the bar. I started breaking down the blunt when my phone rang. I turned my head and looked down at the phone. It was Quan calling. I knew that he had something for me because it was barely seven in the morning and he was calling.

"What up, Q? I know you got something for a nigga," I said, putting the call on speaker.

"Yo, G. I looked over the footage and it captured everything, my nigga. That bitch did Nova dirty as hell—"

I cut him off mid-sentence, "Who did her dirty? That nigga Kelvin? What did he do to her, Q?" I was throwing questions at him left to right. I didn't give him a chance to answer one damn question.

"G! If you would shut the fuck up for a minute, I would be able to tell you what the fuck I saw. Damn, nigga! Just let me talk for once!" he screamed into the phone.

"A'ight, fam. Go ahead," I started, breaking down the weed and then loaded the blunt up. I knew at that point I was gonna need that shit when he said what he had to say.

"The video showed Nova walking into the store. She was in there for about a half hour or so before she came back out. She was placing her purchases in the back seat when that bitch Ziva walked up on her with a bat in hand. She waited for Nova to raise up out of the car and hit her in the head with that damn aluminum bat. Nova fell to the ground and she wasn't moving, G. The bitch had parked her car next to hers, so it didn't take her long to toss her in the trunk."

When Quan said Ziva's bitch ass was the one that did that shit to Nova, I was beyond pissed. That bitch better be like

Casper and get ghost out of this muthafucka' because I better not ever see her ass up close and personal. Shit, she better hope I don't spot her as from a distance either.

"Who helped her ass lift her into the trunk? Was she by herself? Could you see in the fucking car?" I lit the blunt and took a hefty pull off that muthafucka. My adrenaline was on an all-time high. Once again, this weed was not working for me.

"There you go with the back to back questions again. I'm gonna answer every one of them, fam. No one helped her lift sis into the trunk. As a matter of fact, I zoomed all the way into her car and she was alone. The bitch didn't even pull off right away. She sat there and made a phone call."

At that moment, Lady started hitting the bell that I had attached to the patio door. I taught her how to ring it when she was just a month old. I got up and opened the door. I waited for Lady to get all the way into the house and closed and locked it. I walked back to the bar, grabbing my phone before I went to the kitchen to fill her a bowl with water and food. Quan was rustling papers around on the other end of the phone, then he started talking again.

"The information that Monica gave us about Ziva panned out for the most part. She hasn't been to her apartment as far as Gino could tell. I had that nigga go to her shit and break in. The bitch don't know the meaning of banks because she had twenty five large in a shoebox in her closet. I'll get that to you when I see you. So, that tells me that she got paid for something, my nigga. She wasn't driving the car that Monica said she had. She copped a new whip. She has a Black 2017 Nissan Maxima. I got the license plate number, as well. I ran the tags and they came back belonging to her. I didn't get any hits on her phone, so she may have gotten a new number. But we will not give up, G. This shit may take a little bit of time."

"Time! Too much fuckin' time has already lapsed, my nigga! There's no telling what those two muthafuckas are doing to her right now!" I felt the tears trying to escape my eyes. I was fighting them tooth and nail, but that shit was burning.

"I'm gonna try to get in touch with that nigga Conte just to see what he knows. I gave you all that I have, but that don't mean I'm gonna quit. This is an all day, all night mission, my nigga. I'm on this shit until we get her back if it kills me," Quan said with conviction.

"You gave me plenty to go off, man. Thank you for that. We know that Ziva was the one that snatched Nova and, at some point, that nigga Kelvin took over. I'm gonna go out in these streets and let these muthafuckas see my face. I haven't been out and about in a while. It's time to remind these niggas who run these muthafuckin' streets. Thanks again, fam. I appreciate all that you are doing. I'm about to get off here so I can get on this shit. Hit my line if you hear anything else. Be easy," I said, ending the call.

***

After getting off the phone with Quan, I headed to the shower to get my hygiene together. I turned the hot water on and proceeded to brush my teeth. Looking down, I saw Nova's toothbrush and all her hair products lined up on the counter. She had practically moved in since the shooting at her house. I had put the house up for sale, but we were still waiting to hear from the realtor. I touched up my goatee and washed my face before stepping into the steamy water. I jumped out quick as hell because I almost gave myself third degree burns. That water was hot! Adjusting the temperature, I stepped back in, washing my body three times and getting out. I grabbed the black bath towel that was hanging on the rack and dried off.

I walked into my bedroom and grabbed my phone, finding Scony's number and hit him up. I waited patiently for him to answer. He finally picked up, sounding tired as fuck.

"What's up, brah? What's going on?" he asked.

"I got some news about what went down with Nova. Quan called and told me what he found on the video footage. Ziva hit her in the head with a bat and put her in the trunk of her car. I can't stop myself from thinking the worst man. He said she wasn't moving and that worries me."

"Calm down, G. What do you wanna do? I'm down for whateva. All you have to do is say the word and I'm there," Scony said.

"I think we need to go out in these streets, brah. We have to get some answers. I wanna check out the address where Tonio followed Ziva too, as well. We probably can find something there, as well. Finding that nigga's sister is a must, too. I know she didn't have shit to do with none of this, but he made her and anybody else a target."

"I feel you on that, fam. Let me get myself together. Give me two hours and we can roll out," he said.

"Nah, it's too early. I will hit Quan back up and tell him to look into finding out more on Kelvin's sister. When he gets back with me, I'll hit you up. After that, it's on, my nigga. Until then, be easy," I said, ending the call.

I called Quan up letting him know what I needed him to do He was on it before I got off the phone. I took that time to call Nova's phone to see if it would be answered, but it went straight into voicemail. I tossed the phone on the bed and crawled under the covers, going back to sleep.

I woke up to the sound of my phone ringing. I had to search for it because I didn't know where it was. Finally locating it, I picked it up before the voicemail did it for me.

"Yo!" I answered.

"Hey, G. I got some news for you, my nigga." It was Quan on the other end. "I found out who his sister is, fam. Her name is Bonita Banks, but everybody calls her BB. She has three kids and she lives on the westside on North Ave and Laramie. Her kids go to John Hay Elementary School, literally right down the street from her crib, my nigga. We can catch her picking them up this afternoon."

"How the fuck are we gonna do that? We don't know what this bitch looks like." I said, not trying to hide the frustration in my voice.

"I know what she looks like. You will, too, when I shoot the pic to your phone. Yo' ass knows that I don't deliver any news without having all of the information to pass on," he said, laughing. That's why this nigga was on my team, he was thorough as fuck.

"That's what the fuck I'm talking about. Thanks, nigga. I owe you big time."

"You don't owe me shit. This is what the fuck I get paid for. Plus, you know with this shit right here, I will do it for free. You don't go all out for anyone you don't care about. Nova is family, nigga, and I want to find her as bad as you do. So, with that being said, I'm out," he said, hanging up.

I shot Scony and Tonio a text about the moves that we were gonna make later that afternoon. I sent them the address and time to be at the school, along with the picture of Bonita. Both responded with the "thumbs up" emoji. I sat there with my eyes closed for a minute, then I sent a text to a couple of the goons, as well. I wanted the school surrounded. She would not get the chance to get away from us.

I finally got up to get dressed at twelve-thirty in the afternoon. I pulled out a black Nike jogging suit. I paired it with some black AirMax and was ready to go. I wasn't trying to get spiffy to go talk to a bitch that I may have to yoke up. I had to

55

hurry and make my way to the westside. It was already a quarter to one and the school let out at two forty-five. I wanted everyone to be in position before the bell rang. I had a goon in the front of her apartment and another in the back. I would be in the front of the school, Scony would be on the north side, Tonio would take up the back and the lil' goon, Suave, will be on the south side of the building. I had all bases covered to get this bitch.

I grabbed my keys and checked to see if my bitch was in place on my hip. I walked to the kitchen and into the garage. Seeing Nova's car only pissed me off, but I had to check my attitude. I didn't want to go into this maliciously with the sister. I was going to try to talk to her ass first. I would just have to see how that worked out for me.

Once I pulled out of the garage, I made sure that the door went down completely before I pulled off. I burned rubber trying to get to the expressway in record time. Once I hit that bitch, it was on. I took off like I was in the Batmobile. I grabbed my phone and called Scony to see what his location was.

"Yo! Where ya at?" I asked him.

"I'm en route. I also made sure that everyone else were, as well. So, all we need to do is get there and sit. This shit will be over soon, brah. Sis will be home before you know it. I'll see you in a bit. One," he said, ending the call.

I took that opportunity to think about what I would do once this shit was over. So many thoughts ran through my mind putting a much-needed smile on my face. I saw nothing, but great things coming out of this thing with Nova and myself. I know that I wanted her to be there right by my side for eternity.

I pulled up to the school at one forty-five. I hit my niggas up so we could talk before everything went down. But before I could pick up my phone, it started ringing.

"Yeah," I said, answering the phone. It was Griff, the lil' nigga that I had watching the apartment.

"Aye, G. I see baby girl walking down the street. What do you want me to do?" he asked.

"Grab that bitch. We may as well get her ass now because there will be too many people at the school to do that shit unnoticed. There's no better time than now. Hit me when you got her."

I hit up the others in a mass text to meet me down the street at the bitch crib. While I was driving, I got a text that he had her in the car. I didn't bother to reply, I just kept going. I spotted his ride and he drove down Laramie towards the expressway. Then my phone rang. "Yo," I said, while continuing to drive.

"What's the word, nigga? I'm about to take this shorty to grab something to eat before I take her back to the school to pick up her kids. I may have to postpone the meeting, my nigga,"

I knew that he was trying to see where I wanted him to go. "Take her to the trap in K-Town. We can question her ass there. Good job. I'll see you in a minute."

I sent a text to the others letting them know the plan. When I pulled up to the trap, everyone else pulled up back to back. I only wanted her to tell me where her brother was. I knew that it wasn't going to be that easy, but I was willing to give her the benefit of the doubt. We all walked into the trap and ole girl was sitting on a stool. She turned when she saw us walk in and started fumbling with her coat.

"Hey, BB. How are you doing, baby girl?" Tonio asked, staring at her with a smirk on his face.

"Do I know you? I don't think I've ever met any of you before and how do you know my name?" she asked, looking around.

"You don't know us, but we know of you. We knew enough to track yo' ass down, but you didn't answer my question, sweetie. I asked how are you doing?" Tonio repeated the question.

"I'm about to go. I see that y'all niggas are on some bull-shit and I don't want no parts of this," she said, standing up and attempting to walk past us. When she figured out that she wasn't going anywhere, she started trying to cry.

"Please don't rape me. I was just going to pick my kids up from school. Let me go, please," she cried.

"Rape? Ain't nobody about to rape yo' ass. Do we look like rapists, bitch?" Scony asked her through clenched teeth. "I'm not about to play with yo' ass. Where the fuck his yo' bitch ass brother? And I'm not talking about the ones that's eating dirt either."

"This shit is about Kelvin? I haven't heard from his stupid ass since he cremated my damn mama without talking it over with me first. I don't know where his ass is. He has been hanging out with that hoe Ziva lately. I lost all respect for that nigga when he did that shit to Sabrina and got my mama killed. I really hope y'all didn't think that I would put my life on the line for that selfish muthafucka. If I see his ass, I would call y'all myself. Fuck him! He is no longer a brother of mine."

For some odd reason, I believed her. She was mad as hell and the disgust that was shown for him seemed genuine. She wasn't going to get away that easily, though. I had to put some fear in her ass.

"I see the hatred that you have for your brother now, but I'm here to let you know that if I find out otherwise, your kids are gonna be orphans. Your brother is gonna die before it's

58

said and done. He fucked up when he did what he did. He has to pay the piper with his life and I don't have a problem eliminating his entire family to bring his bitch ass out of hiding. There will be eyes on you and yo' kids at all times. Don't try no slick shit because I'll have one hollow tip bullet pierce your skull before you blink. What I want you to do is call this number when he shows up. If you hate him as much as you say, then it wouldn't be a problem. But if he is seen coming out of your muthafuckin' house and the phone to this number don't ring, yo' ass is gonna rest with the rest of yo' family, bitch," I said, writing the number down and handing it to her.

"Take her ass back to the school to get her kids and you better keep ya mouth closed. Is that understood?" I asked her, staring into her eyes. She shook her head up and down, and I moved out of the way to let her past. Griff grabbed her arm leading her out of the door.

This trap was one that we no longer used. It was in another nigga's name, so I didn't give a fuck about it.

"Burn this muthafucka down just in case she wanted to call the Po Po to tell her story. Griff will be the one to keep an eye on this bitch. I truthfully don't think she is gonna say anything, but you can never be sure about these hoes," I said, walking back to my car. "Meet me on the Nine. We have some shit to figure out." I got in my ride and peeled off.

Meesha

Chapter 6

Monica

Jade and I sat up all evening trying to find ways to keep our minds off the situation with Nova. It was hard because that's our sister and couldn't no one tell us different. I had been checking the Find My Phone app every five minutes, but there hadn't been any type of activity on it at all. The guys hadn't called to give any updates, so I was guessing they hadn't found out anything new.

I tried calling Ziva's phone, but the number had been disconnected. I swear I can't wait to see that bitch in the streets. I've known this bitch for years and didn't know about anyone in her inner circle because it was all about the four of us. Her family is in Arizona and she don't fuck with them anyway, so I knew she wasn't there. That bitch was still here in the Chi, but where? I had never heard of her hanging tough with any other people except dudes. But many of them just wanted to fuck her hoe ass, throw her some money and lead her to the door with a wet ass.

"Monica, are you all right over there? You have been quiet for the past twenty minutes. You're not even paying attention to the movie," Jade said, turning her head to look at me. She was wrapped up in a throw blanket up to her chin.

The weather in Chicago wasn't no joke. It was November and cold as fuck. There wasn't any snow, but that hawk was out, baby. I had the heat on, but I think these muthafuckas need to insulate these damn windows.

"I'm fine. Just trying to figure out where the hell Ziva could be. Her ass knows what's going on. I'll put money on that. Nothing is coming to my mind though and it's frustrating

61

as hell. It's the first day of the month. Nova must be found before Thanksgiving, Jade. If she isn't, I will not have anything to be thankful for," I said with a tear running down my cheek.

"Mo, we have to keep a positive mindset. In my heart, I know Nova is alive. She's coming back to us. Shit, she's coming back for G's ass! Fuck you thought? That nigga ain't about to sit around twiddling his thumbs. He is gonna find her ass or die trying, believe that shit. Stop all that crying. She's good." Jade sat up to hug me and her phone rang. She jumped up fast and sprinted to the island in the kitchen.

"Scony, did y'all find out anything?" she said into the phone.

When she mentioned Scony's name, I turned all the way around so I could look directly in her face. Her face fell into a deep frown and she shook her head no, indicating that they hadn't found out anything. We hadn't heard from them since this time yesterday, but we tried not to dwell on it. We just chilled up until now.

"Okay, I'll see you when you get here. I'll be ready," she said, pressing the end button and laying her phone down.

"They found Nova's car at Michaels yesterday. They have the surveillance footage, but they have to see what Quan comes up with when he looks at it. G is in a fucked up midframe right now. He found all the tests and the items she purchased in the car. They found out some other things, but he didn't go into detail about it. But Tonio and Scony is on their way here," she explained, while walking around gathering her things.

Stepping into the kitchen, she looked around and started putting the Tupperware bowls of food in the fridge. We ended up eating the food today. We didn't touch any of it last night. We just went to sleep.

"Jade, you don't have to do that. I will take care of it."

"Girl, bye. You need to be getting up to take a shower so you will be ready when that man comes through that door. I see how he looks at your ass. He's getting some pussy tonight," she laughed. All I could do was shake my head at her ass.

I stood from the chaise that I was lounging in and headed to my bedroom. Jade was correct. Antonio was going to get all in my love tonight. I needed something to take my mind off everything that was going on around me. What better way than a long sex session? I went into the bathroom and turned the water on in the shower. I needed the water to be hotter than usual because I had to relax a little bit.

I took off my clothes and stepped into the steam-filled shower. Instantly closing my eyes, the water hit me from my head to my feet. The tears started flowing, I was hurting so bad for my friend. I kept asking myself why was she going through all of this shit. She didn't deserve any of it.

I didn't know how long I was in the shower, but I hadn't washed one part of my body. I reached for my loofah at the same time the shower curtain was pulled back. My arm fell to my side and I was wondering who could possibly be invading my fuckin' privacy.

"Are you all right, baby? I heard you crying when I stepped into your bedroom."

I turned and there stood Antonio in a black wife beater and some black jeans that was fitting just right, showcasing his bowed legs. His caramel skin was the perfect shade to complement my dark skin. He was so sexy standing there doing absolutely nothing.

"I'm not okay," I said, breaking down again. He started taking off his Tims, then his socks and his jeans. He didn't bother taking off his boxers or his wife beater. He stepped into

63

the shower and wrapped his arms around me. I laid my head on his chiseled chest and cried like a baby. He reached back and grabbed my loofah and the body wash that I had in the caddy.

Lathering the loofah, he started washing me from head to toe. I felt helpless, but I didn't have the energy to protest. When he got to my love box and started washing me, I let out the deepest moan. He continued to wash that spot over and over until I came long and hard. That action alone made me feel ten pounds lighter.

"Turn around, baby. I need to wash your back. The water is starting to cool off," he said, never taking his eyes off me.

I turned like he asked and rested my arms on the shower walls. He started washing my back, ass and the back of my legs. He raised my left foot and washed that as well, doing the same with the right. I hadn't been catered to like this in forever. It felt good, but my emotions wouldn't let me fully enjoy what he was doing. He rinsed my entire body and started massaging my calves.

Running his hands up and down my legs, he lifted my left leg, propping it on the edge of the tub. In a split second, I felt his wet tongue doing figure eights on my clit. I collapsed against the shower wall, my legs were shaking uncontrollably. I was losing my footing, so he grabbed me around my waist and turned me around. He stood up and pinned me against the tile. Lifting me up with my back against the wall, he looked at me with an eyeful of lust. His shirt was plastered to his chest and his muscles were protruding.

He kissed me fully on my lips. The taste of my juices was very sweet. Our tongues danced for a few minutes before he pulled away, kissing his way back down my body. Going in head first, he sucked the soul out of my kitty like he was sucking from a straw. My breath got caught in my throat, I thought

I was going to die from asphyxiation. Slipping two fingers in my snatch, he was performing the 'come here' motion in my tunnel and sucking hard on my pearl at the same time. My stomach muscles clenched tightly. I took a deep breath and all my sweet nectar found its way down his throat.

Antonio lowered me to the floor of the tub and washed me once more. He got out and disrobed, dropping his wet clothes into the sink. He grabbed my plush bath towel off the rack and walked back to the shower. Turning the water off, he wrapped me in the towel and picked me up. He carried me to the bedroom, laying me down. He dried me off completely and covered me with the blanket. Before my head could touch the pillow, I was out like a light.

***

I woke up feeling like a breath of fresh air. That tongue lashing that Tonio gave me last night put me right to sleep. I had never had any man eat my cookies like that in my entire life. To make the night even more exciting, he let me sleep for a couple hours. Then he was right back feasting, waking me up to the most exhilarating orgasm I have ever had. When I say this man had me squirting all over his face, I thought he would need to put on goggles and scuba gear. He was literally deep-sea diving in my shit.

I was holding on to the sheets like my life depended on it. His tongue was so long that when he licked me from my ass to the top of my pussy, he didn't have to move his tongue very far. He had this thing that he did with his tongue that had me squealing like a pig. Somehow, he made his tongue curl, wrapping it around my pearl and holding on tight as hell while he sucked on it. I came so hard, my body elevated off the bed. I can honestly say that I was stuck from head alone. If he was serious about this shit, I'm all in because if he kept putting it down like that, bitches better be aware. Once he's mine, I'm not letting him go.

Sniffing the air, my stomach started growling from the aroma of bacon being cooked. I know this man is not in my kitchen cooking. A man that can cook is sexy. I got up and went into the bathroom to take care of my hygiene. I had dried up slob on the corner of my mouth and shit, I hope he didn't look me in the face this morning. I was embarrassed thinking about it. He was the reason I didn't have any muscle control in my face.

I jumped in the shower and washed away all the sins of last night. The visuals were embedded in my head, making me tremble with every stroke of the loofah. I would never look at it as just a bathing tool again. I hurried to wash and hopped out of the shower.

Entering my bedroom, I stopped in my tracks. There were rose petals all over the room with a dozen roses sitting on the night stand. I walked over to the flowers and picked up the card that was attached. Opening the card, I began to read.

Good morning, baby.

You are a very special woman. I am willing to wait however long it takes for you to be mine. I know you are wondering why I didn't try to take it further. I'm looking for more than sex, baby. I'm looking for forever. So when you are ready, let me know. But until then, I'm gonna treat you like the Queen that you are. I need to let you know that you taste better than the strawberries that I had this morning. I'm looking forward to showering you with different types of love, baby.

Tonio

I held the card to my chest. I couldn't stop smiling. Tonio walked into the bedroom with only his jeans on. This man was beautiful and I could look at him all day. He walked over to the standup meal tray and placed a plate on top. He went all out with the breakfast. There were pancakes, eggs, bacon, sausage, toast, grits and a tall glass of orange juice, staring up at me. I looked at him, placing my hands on my hips.

"Thank you so much for the flowers and the breakfast, Tonio, but who the hell is gonna eat all of this?" I asked.

He laughed as he walked towards me. "You are, sexy. I don't like a woman that's afraid to eat. I like a woman that has meat on her bones, that thick shit," he said, looking my body up and down while licking his lips.

"Tonio, I just lost a lot of weight. I'm not trying to gain it back. I can't eat all of this."

"I don't know why you felt you had to lose weight. I'm quite sure you were just as beautiful then as you are now. But I know that had to do with a fuck nigga, one who didn't know how to appreciate a jewel while he had her. Shit is gonna change for you, Miss Mo. I'm gonna make sure that confidence of yours stays on Queen status. Watch me work, baby. Now sit yo' ass down and enjoy your breakfast." I sat down and I can honestly say it was very good.

"Aren't you gonna eat anything?" I said in between bites.

"Nah, ma. I had plenty to eat last night and I had a couple of strawberries that didn't have shit on the nectar you served up," he said, smirking while heading to the bathroom. All I could do was blush, while taking a sip of juice. My throat dried up instantly after that statement.

Meesha

Chapter 7

Scony

When me and Tonio made it to Monica's, Jade was sitting on the couch watching TV. I walked over to her and kissed her cheek. She was looking so sad and I didn't know how to make her feel better at all. I was going to do my best to cheer her up before I went out in the streets to tear shit up. I must go check on Lovely. She had been doing great in the treatment center. I'm very proud of her. Since Malikhi's death, she had been pushing to do better. I decided I would go check on her first thing in the morning.

"What's up, Jade? Where's Mo?" Antonio asked.

"Hey, Tonio. She's in her room. She may be in the shower, though." He walked to the back of the house in search of Monica, leaving us in the living room.

Jade was sitting quietly, staring straight ahead. I sat next to her and wrapped her in my arms, her body relaxed instantly. I made circles on her back with my hands. I had never enjoyed a woman like this without thinking of sex. I wanted to change my approach with this one. She's not one of these females that is out for material shit. I believe she's a keeper. Time will tell, though.

"Everything is gonna be all right, Jade. Nova is coming home. I'll make that promise to you myself. I know it's hard to put all of this to the side, but you're gonna have to in order to go on about your life. I'm not saying don't be worried, but don't worry yourself sick. Let's get out of here so you can relax," I said, patting her leg.

She lifted her head off my chest and pushed up off the couch. I grabbed the remote and turned the TV off. Watching her gather her things, I knew that I would cherish her. It's going to be a challenge, but I think I'll be able to complete the mission. Walking to where she was standing, I held my hand out for her bags and leaned in to give her a peck on her lips.

"Thank you for being here for me. I appreciate it, Demarius Jones." She was looking at me with admiration and a smile formed on my lips instantly.

"No thanks needed, babe. That's what I'm supposed to do, be there when you need me the most. Now come on so I can take you home, beautiful."

"I don't want to go home. I want to go with you," she said, walking to the door. I was surprised that she wanted to come home with me, but I had to make sure I continued to be a gentleman. Every time I had sex with a woman without trying to get to know her first, it continued to be just sex from that point on. Jade deserved more than that and I was willing to give her that and more.

"That's fine. We can go to my place. Are you hungry?" I asked her, while we walked out the door. She turned, taking her keys out of her purse to lock it before responding.

"No, I'm not hungry, I don't have an appetite at all."

"You have to eat, Jade. Let's roll on over to Goose Island Shrimp House."

"Goose Island! I haven't had any of their seafood in a long time, but it's so far away, Demarius. It's like thirty minutes away!" she said in a squeaky voice that was making my ears ring.

"It doesn't matter how far it is. I want some and so do you. I can tell by the way your eyes lit up when I mentioned it. Let's go, girl," I said, walking to my car and opening the door.

I held the door open and waited for her to get to the car. I stepped to the side so she could get inside. When she was situated, I helped her put her seatbelt on and whispered lowly in her ear, "You better be lucky I like yo' ass. There are very few people that can call me by my real name, but I like the way it falls from your pretty lips. Now let me taste them." I captured her bottom lip in my mouth and sucked on it softly.

I pecked them once more and stood up and closed the door. As I walked to the driver's side of the car, I looked through the window and her eyes were still closed. I chuckled to myself. I got in and started up the car, backing out of the parking spot. We were driving for a nice minute when my phone rang. I leaned over to get it out of my pocket. I hated talking on the phone while driving, so I handed the phone to Jade and asked her to answer it. She looked at me, then back down to the phone.

"Are you sure you want me to answer this?" she asked.

"I wouldn't have asked you to answer it if I didn't want you to do just that. I don't say things I don't mean, Jade. Remember that, sweetie." By the time we finished with the uncertainties, the phone stopped ringing.

"I only asked because it was someone named Nicassy. I don't have time to be arguing with your female friends. I have too much going on with my friend being gone. I don't have a problem having you pull up on these hoes because they didn't know how to mind their mouths. It wouldn't have shit to do with you because you're not my man. It will be the lack of respect on their part."

I looked over at her for a second and returned my attention to the road. She said that shit calm as fuck. She didn't even look like the type of woman that would say some shit like that.

"Nicassy isn't someone that I've ever fucked with like that. She's like a little sister to me." I was trying to explain shit to her, but all she wanted to do was run her damn mouth.

"You don't have to explain anything to me, Scony. That's your business. I'm not your—" I cut her ass off before she could get beside herself. I knew she was in her feelings because she didn't call me by my government.

"Shut yo' ass up for a minute, Jade! I know I don't *have* to explain anything to you. I choose to do that shit. Hell nawl, you ain't my woman, but by the time I'm finished with yo' ass you will be. Get ready to wear that muthafuckin' title. Ain't no bitch ever had it, but I want you to."

Her ass was sitting there silent as fuck, blushing. I bet her damn thong was soaking wet. Her ass had been fucking around with these fuck niggas. She better get ready because ain't shit soft about me.

"Don't cut me off no mo'. Now, like I was saying, Nicassy is like my little sister. She has been a part of my family since we were kids. Her mom was on that shit bad and my grandmother took her in at the age of twelve. She has been my sister ever since. When I came up in the game, I took care of her the same way I did my biological sisters. When the twins and my grandmother moved to Atlanta, it was only me and her in the Chi. Hell yeah, we still look out for each other. So she ain't a threat, period," I said, glancing in her direction briefly.

As soon as I finished that statement, my phone rang again. I looked over at Jade and she had a smirk on her face. She slid the button to answer the phone with her eyes trained on me. Placing the phone to her ear pausing, she said, "Hello."

She repeated the greeting and waited. Shaking her head, she took the phone from her ear and put it on speaker.

"Who the fuck is this? Scony, don't let nan bitch answer his phone. You need to be telling me who the fuck you are. As a matter of fact, where his ass at?"

That was this female that I was smashing on a regular. Damn, I couldn't fuck shit up with her just in case this shit with me and Jade didn't work out. Her pussy was grade A and she sucked dick like a vacuum. Her suction was everything.

My python swelled up just thinking about it. I pulled up to the restaurant and parked, then looked over at Jade. Her eyes were trained on my ass like a sharp shooter.

"Ummmm, don't get quiet now. You already answered my man's phone. Now, where is he?"

Her man? I never gave this broad any kind of title. Shit, in my mind her name was Suction Susan. I had to deaden that shit before this girl went crazy. I had just told Jade what I was aiming for and here is this shit. Well, I guess I won't be fucking on this one no more.

"Yo, shorty. Pipe that shit down and show some muthafuckin' respect. I don't recall you ever paying a bill this way while you're trying to check somebody about my shit. Make that yo' last time calling my girl out of her name. What we had going on now is over. Shit, I haven't smashed yo' ass in a minute no way. But you won't have to worry about me hittin' you up no mo' because I'll be blocking yo' ass when this conversation concludes. Let me hear it. What's the nature of yo' call?

"Fuck you, Scony! You said all I needed to hear. You don't have to worry about me calling you anymore." She hung up the phone and the car was eerily quiet.

"There is gonna be a lot of that happening from here on out. I'm getting rid of them all. I already know where I wanna be," I said, looking Jade in her eyes.

"We'll see. Now let's get in here and get this food. You and your hoes made me hungry," she said, getting out the car.

"Yo' ass was already hungry. Stop frontin'," I said, smacking her on her ass.

***

When we finally got to my house, my stomach was damn near in my back. I took off my coat, hanging it in the hall closet. I put the many bags of food on the table and went to wash my hands. Jade was already in the bathroom washing hers. She just threw her coat on the back of the couch. Her ass is going to hang that muthafucka up though. That's not how I operate around here. I am OCD like a muthafucka, I hate shit being out of place. But I'm not cleaning up after a grown ass nigga either.

"Jade, why the hell you throw your coat on my couch and not hang it in the closet? I can't stand that shit. I like things to be in order. I hate clutter, bae," I explained to her.

"Demarius, why didn't you just hang the coat up? I mean, damn, it's not a big deal, but okay. This is your house, your rules," she said, rolling her eyes.

"It's not about me having rules or if it's my house, Jade. I like to have a clutter-free home. This is my comfort zone. When you start putting things where it don't belong, it will build up and that's how you accumulate clutter. That's all I'm saying."

Jade's house is very clean. I don't have to question her cleanliness at all. Believe me if her shit was a mess, we wouldn't even be able to rock. That shit is learned early on and if she hasn't grasped that shit by adulthood, she never would. And there wouldn't be a future for us. I didn't give a fuck how much I was feeling her ass.

"Wash your hands, boo, so we can eat. I'm about to hang my coat up, as well," she said, drying her hands on a paper towel, walking out of the bathroom.

When I walked back into the kitchen, she had the food laid out on the table. This woman ordered jumbo shrimp, fish and chips, frog legs, french fries, crab salad, calamari and fried clams. For somebody that wasn't hungry, she sure ordered enough food like she was one of those damn kids on one of those "Feed the Kids" ads. But I was about to fuck this shit up! She fixed me a plate with a little bit of everything on it with mild and hot sauce on the side.

"Damn, bae. This shit looks good as hell. Do you want to eat in here or in the living room?" I asked her, while popping a frog leg in my mouth. I had never had frog legs, but this shit tasted like chicken. She just started some shit with this one. I would be ordering these from now on.

"With your OCD issues, I think we should eat right here at the kitchen table. I would hate to get crumbs on your sofa," she said, chuckling.

I didn't see nothing funny to be honest, but I was going to let her have her little comedy moment. I grabbed the remote off the island and pressed the button to reveal the sixty-inch television I had hidden in a cabinet in the corner. The doors to the cabinet were opened with a push of a button.

"That is so nice! I never thought to have a TV in the kitchen," Jade said in between bites of her shrimp.

"Yeah, it is nice. I had it installed so when I have guests over we would have entertainment in every room, bathrooms included."

"Tell me why you have this big ass house Demarius. This is too much space for one person," she said, waiting on my response.

I found the movie *John Wick* on the Firestick and pressed play. Laying the remote down, I picked up a piece of jumbo shrimp and took a bite. Once I swallowed the food, I answered her question.

"I chose this house because I loved the layout and it's beautiful. As far as the size, I thought about my future when I made this purchase. I imagined a house full of kids, a dog and a Queen that will make it a home. It's in the beginning stages right now, but I know that my vision is gonna become a reality in due time," I said, never taking my eyes off her.

75

Jade sat there nodding her head, taking in what I had said. I was stealing glances at the TV and stuffing my face. My phone starting ringing and I looked at Jade. She still had my phone. She wiped her hands with a napkin and answered it.

"Hello," she said, listening to the person on the other end.

"I'm sorry. I must have the wrong number. I was looking for Demarius," the female said.

"This is Demarius' phone. May I ask who's calling?"

I could tell that Jade was uncomfortable answering my phone, but I had nothing to hide, so I wasn't worried about anything.

"This can't possibly be Demarius' phone. He don't let anyone answer his shit. Who is this?"

"This is Jade, his woman. Now, may I ask who's calling for the second time," she asked calmly.

"This is his sister, MaKayla. Now where is my brother! I don't have time for this back and forth shit you have me going through. If he is there, put him on the fuckin' phone, please!" she yelled.

Jade put the phone on speaker and pushed it towards me, continuing to eat her food. She was nonchalant about the entire conversation and was done with it. I wiped my hands and grabbed the phone. Twin Kay was displayed on the screen.

"Hey, Kay baby. What's up?" I asked, speaking into the phone.

"Why the hell didn't you answer when Nicassy called yo' high yellow ass? This is not the time for you to be having someone screening yo' fuckin calls, my nigga. You ain't been doing that shit, don't start now," she said, sniffling.

"Hold up! What's wrong, Kay?"

MaKayla was my youngest twin sister by three minutes. She and her twin, MaKenzie, were tougher than me at times and rarely cried about anything. To hear the sadness and anger in her voice sent chills down my spine.

"I had Nicassy call you because I couldn't at the time. Grandma had a massive heart attack, Scony. She didn't make it. We are at the hospital now and Kenzie is a mess. They pronounced her dead an hour ago. She was all we had left, man. What am I supposed to do without my grandma?" Kayla was crying like a little baby and there was nothing I could do to console her.

"MaKayla! I will be down there as soon as I can get the jet fueled up, baby girl. Stay strong for me, sis. I'm on my way. I'm sorry that I didn't answer the phone. I could be there already if I had, but I'm on my way, baby girl. Text me the information I need to see her. I know that she will be taken to the morgue, but I must see her for myself. Let me get off this phone so I can get things in motion. I'll see you soon and I love you, sis." I said, disconnecting the phone.

Jade sat there with the saddest look on her face while I held my hands under my chin. The room was quiet for about ten minutes then she broke the silence.

"I'm so sorry about your grandmother, Demarius. Is there anything I can do for you? I'll go with you if you need me to."

"Nah, shorty. I don't know how long I will be gone and I don't want you to miss work because of me. I'm going down there to get my grandma and bring her body back here. She don't know them muthafuckas in the A. She deserves to be buried at home, right here in Chicago." I was feeling bad because I hadn't been down to see them in a few months, but my grandma knew what I was into.

I talked to her every day and shit was good, then out of the blue she had a damn heart attack. My grandma would have been eighty-five years old on December twelfth. This was about to be one fucked up holiday season. Nova is still missing

77

and now I had to make the arrangements to bury my granny. What else could go wrong?

I picked up the phone and called Chico so he could have the jet gassed up and ready to go. He said it would be ready in an hour. At that point, the tears were threatening to fall from my eyes. I didn't know how I was going to deal with this. It was like déjà vu all over again. First, my mama, then Malikhi. Now, it's my granny. This shit was hard on a nigga.

Contemplating if I should call G or not, I picked up my phone and put it back down. G is going through so much trying to get Nova back, but he will beat my ass if I didn't tell him what was going on with Granny. She damn near raised his ass when we were younger. He was always at my crib. I picked my phone up and dialed his number. The phone rang several times before he picked up.

"What up, Scon? You got some news for me, bro?" G didn't sound like himself and it worried me.

"I have some news, but it's not the news you want to hear. I haven't heard anything else about Nova, but I got a call from Kayla. Granny passed away tonight, G. I have Chico gassing up the jet as we speak so I can go down there. I know you can't leave right now with the shit that's going on with sis, but I understand." I got all that out in one breath, my heart beating uncontrollably because I was in disbelief.

"Damn, bro! Don't tell me that shit, man! I'm gonna call Tonio and Quan so they can hold down the fort until we return. They can handle shit here with no problem. Hopefully when we get back, they will have something to tell me about Nova. But there's no way I'm letting you go down there by yourself. Shit, that's my grandma, too, nigga. What time will the jet be ready?"

"In a little under an hour. I'll meet you at Midway Airport. I have to call Lovely and let her know what's going on."

"Okay, fam. See you then. One."

As soon as the call disconnected, I dialed Lovely's phone and it went straight to voicemail. Maybe she had it turned off. I'll try again later. I took that time to call my Aunt Sarah. This is going to be hard for her, as well.

"Hey, Auntie. How are you?" I asked when she answered the phone.

"Demarius, what's wrong? And you better not say nothing."

I couldn't get the words out to save my life. They were stuck in my throat.

"Demarius, are you still there?" My aunt was panicking. I knew I had to say something quick.

"Um, Auntie, Grandma Liz passed away tonight. She had a massive heart attack. MaKayla called and told me. I'm on my way there in a few to see her and make arrangements to have her brought back here," I said, fighting back the tears.

"Oh my God! Not my mama! I just talked to her earlier and she said she was doing fine. Do you mind if I come, too?"

"Auntie, pack quickly. I have to get to this airport as soon as possible. I'll pick you up in twenty minutes. Oh yeah, have you talked to Lovely? I tried calling, but her phone is going straight to voicemail."

"Let me pack and I'll tell you about that shit in the car. I'll see you soon," my aunt said before hanging up.

I couldn't catch a break. I went to the kitchen and told Jade what the plan was. She was going to ride with me and hold on to my whip until I returned. Now I have less than ten minutes to pack and get out of here.

***

I packed in record time and me and Jade was out the door. On the way to my aunt's house, the car was quiet. Jade kept stealing glances at me, but I kept my eyes on the road. A couple of minutes later, I felt her hand grab mine, intertwining our fingers. I squeezed her hand and lifted it to my lips, kissing the back of it.

"Demarius, I'm sorry that we didn't answer the phone when we were in the car. If we would have answered, you would have known about your grandmother earlier."

"You have nothing to be sorry about, bae. If we had answered the phone when Nicassy called, she still would have been gone. Nothing would have changed the outcome, so please don't blame yourself for this," I said to her as I pulled up to my aunt's house.

Before I could get out of the car, Aunt Sarah was coming out with her luggage in hand. I climbed out and walked toward her meeting her halfway. I grabbed her luggage and started walking back to the car. The trunk popped and I smiled because Jade was the first woman to do anything like that without being asked to do so. She got out of the car and attempted to get in the backseat.

"Hello, I'm Jade. You can ride up front, ma'am," she said, holding out her hand.

"Nice to meet you, Jade. I'm Sarah. You can stay right where you are. Even if you weren't in the car, I would ride in the back. I don't trust Demarius' driving," she said, ignoring Jade's hand and pulled her in for a hug. They were both laughing at what Aunt Sarah had said. She was telling the truth, though.

"Okay, I keep telling you about talking about my driving. This car wasn't meant to go forty-five miles an hour at any given time. Now, get in the car so we can go," I said, chuckling.

Once everyone was settled in the car, I pulled off heading to the airport.

"Auntie, what's going on with Lovely?" I asked, glancing at her through the rearview mirror.

"Well, I received a call from the rehab facility about four days ago. They informed me that Lovely checked herself out. I asked the woman was she able to do that and she told me yes. The only thing that they can do is try to convince her to stay, unless it was court ordered. They can't force them to stay, so they had to allow her to leave. I have not heard from her at all. Every time I call, I get the voicemail. I have even gone by her apartment and it was empty. She moved out, Demarius." Aunt Sarah sat back and shook her head slowly.

"Damn and she had been doing great for weeks. I wonder what the hell set her back."

"The last time I went to visit her, she was very angry. She kept saying that she was going to get back at that people that killed her baby. I took it as her being off the drugs for a long period of time. Then again, it could be the reason she was back on the streets, smoking her life away."

"We will deal with that when we get back. Right now, I want to concentrate on getting to Atlanta. I have to make sure that my sisters are all right and my granny gets laid to rest like the Queen she was," I said, pulling up on the side of the jet. I saw G standing at the top of the stairs waiting for me, so I got out of the car.

Jade got out and opened the door for Aunt Sarah. "You are a nice one. It's about time he got a woman and left those little hot tailed girls alone. Don't let him try to run you away because he will try to do that shit. I think he fears love. I'll tell you all about that later," she said, giving Jade a hug. Whispering in her ear, she said, "He is going to need you by his side when he returns. Please be there," she said, letting her go.

"I will be. Thank you. I look forward to seeing you again, Miss Sarah."

"You can call me Aunt Sarah, baby," she said, walking toward the jet.

I walked over to Jade and grabbed her around her waist. "I'll call you when I touch down, baby. I want you to watch what's going on around you. I will text you Tonio's number just in case you have any problems. There are plenty of guns in the house in the spare bedroom next to mine. Don't hesitate to use them, if needed. I have to go now, but I will talk to you soon. Drive carefully, baby," I said, kissing her deeply. I didn't want to let her go, but I knew that I had to.

I watched her get into the car and drive off. I watched until I no longer saw the taillights of my car. I missed her already and she had just left.

"Yeah, she is a keeper, Scony. It may be time to throw in your card, nigga," I said to myself, walking up the steps to the jet.

Chapter 8

Kelvin

Something was psychologically wrong with Nova's ass. She was so evil. I had to admit that bitch scared the fuck out of me. It was like she morphed into another person right in front of my eyes. I didn't plan to beat her the way that I did, but her mouth was reckless. She reminded me of how my mama used to talk to my daddy right before he kicked her ass. He used to tell me not to let a bitch talk to me any type of way. He also told me that I should always keep them in check, never allowing them to question my moves. I guess that's why I broke that bitch's jaw, listening to my fucking daddy. Now she couldn't stand my ass and she had every right. But she would be okay if she shut the fuck up sometime.

Ziva left to go hang out with Avah's ass because she called herself being pissed off, but I didn't give a fuck if she was mad. I wasn't going to stand there and watch her try to kill Nova. She was out of her mind for thinking I was going to let shit go down like that. I still loved that woman and she will realize that shit soon.

I walked down the steps to the basement and the sun was shining directly on Nova. She turned her head and looked at me through her one good eye. I really fucked her face up. I felt like shit now since I could see the damage I caused. She looked helpless laying there today. She looked as if she didn't have any more fight in her. I had a bottle of water for her and a turkey on rye sandwich. I knew she had to be hungry. She has been here four days and has yet to eat a single thing.

"How are you feeling, bae?" I asked, sitting the water and sandwich on the nightstand next to the bed.

83

"I'm in so much pain, Kelvin. Why are you doing this to me? What have I done to make you hate me so much? Would you let me get up and use the bathroom? I'm tired of going on myself, then you are cleaning it up. Do you know how degrading that makes me feel? I've been here for days and you won't let me go to the bathroom. I need a shower. Damn!"

I wanted to let her go to the bathroom, but I didn't want her to try some shit and make me fuck her up again. I stood there contemplating what I should do. After a moment of thinking, I decided that I would let her go to the bathroom to take care of all hygienic needs. I went to the linen closet and grabbed two washcloths, a bath towel and one of my tee shirts. I went into the bathroom and set everything on the counter and ran her a bath. Looking around, I made sure there wasn't anything in there that she could kill a nigga with. When I was satisfied that it would be safe, I went back to the bed. I took the pocketknife out of my pocket and reached to cut the tape and stopped.

"If you try anything, I swear I won't hesitate to slit your fuckin' throat. I'm letting you take a bath because I love you, but don't test me, Nova," I said, looking down at her.

"I won't, Kelvin. I just need to go to the bathroom. I don't even want to take a bath now," she said sadly.

"Oh, you're gonna take a bath because I'm getting some of that pussy today. I told you that it would be forever mine and I want to feel every inch of you."

I cut the tape from her legs first and massaged the area. They were bruised and red with little cuts on them. Probably from her trying to get loose without much luck. I walked to the head of the bed and cut her left wrist loose, then walking around to do the same with the right. Her wrist was cut up a little bit, worse than her legs. I helped her stand up and her legs buckled slightly. I made sure I held her firmly around her waist to support her body weight. The piss smell that was on her was strong as fuck, so I had to hold my breath to prevent myself from inhaling it. It smelled like ammonia.

I proceeded to help her take off her clothes and sat her on the toilet. She pissed like a racehorse for three minutes straight. I turned off the water in the tub and turned to help her stand once more. Lowering her into the tub, I gave her both washcloths and a bottle of body wash. I opted to let her soak for a minute so I could change the sheets on the bed. When I turned to leave, she spoke.

"Answer the questions I asked, Kelvin. I really need to know why you are doing this to me?"

"I haven't done anything to you, Nova. Everything that has happened is your fault. I told you not to go out, thinking that you would replace me with the next nigga. Look where that got you. Beat the fuck up! Do you think I enjoyed putting my hands on you? Hell nawl! That shit hurt me mentally as much as it hurt you physically. Then you stay threatening me behind that nigga! I lost my mother because of his punk ass! If this is the way I must keep you in my life, then this is what it will be. You will live the rest of your life as a fucking prisoner playing with me. Now wash yo' ass because I have a run to make. Don't get so happy on the inside because someone will be here to watch yo' ass." I turned and walked out of the bathroom without giving her a chance to respond.

After changing the waterproof mattress pad, sheets and the comforter on the bed, I went into the laundry room and threw the dirty ones in the washer. I looked in on Nova and she had leaned back in the tub with her eyes closed. I let her relax a little bit and I sat in the chair in the corner thinking about who I could trust to come through to sit with her for a couple of hours. No one came to mind because I didn't trust no nigga on the street. Then I remembered that nigga Conte was cool with me. That nigga knew everything that went down with that shit on the Nine and didn't tell a soul. I'll pay his ass five hundred dollars to sit for a couple hours. He would be stupid to say no. Who wouldn't want to make money doing nothing?

I pulled my phone out and hit this nigga up. The phone rang and the nigga sent me to voicemail. I redialed the number and the nigga still didn't answer. I then remembered that I got my number changed and the nigga didn't know the number that I was calling from, so I sent his ass a text.

Me: *Aye, Conte. What up, dude? This Kels. Hit my line, my nigga. I got a proposition for you.*

I got up from the chair and went to the bathroom to check on my boo. When I got to the door, I heard her praying lowly.

"Please, Lord. I'm begging you to get me out of this mess. You have had me going through so much lately and I don't know why. I won't question you, Lord, because you give the toughest battles to your strongest soldiers. I'm trying to stay strong, but I'm breaking. I don't know how much longer I can hold on, Lord. I'm letting you know now, if I get out of here I'm killing these muthafuckas. I'm tired of going through all of this. If I die in the process, save me a seat. You already know my heart and this is the time that you are going to have to forgive me for my sins. In Jesus name, Amen."

I was about to make my presence known when I felt my phone vibrating in my pocket. Easing out of the doorway, I made my way to the opposite side of the basement. I looked at the screen and it was Conte.

"What up, nigga?" I barked in the phone. Nova had me mad as hell with the shit she was spitting to the man upstairs.

"Damn, you were the one that sent me a message to hit you up. You tell me what it is, playa."

"Aye, I need you to do me a solid, my nigga. Would come out to Itasca and keep an eye on somebody for me until I make a run? It will be no more than two or three hours."

"Man, I'm not no babysitter! Where the hell is the mama at?"

"Nigga, it's not a damn baby. It's a whole muthafuckin' woman. I need you to sit with her. I'll pay you five hundred just to sit. I don't need her to be trying to get away while I'm gone, you feel me?"

"Hell nawl, I'm not feeling you. What, you holding the bitch hostage or something? Yo' ass is gonna have to give me a little more to go on," he hesitantly stated.

"I'll tell you more when you get here and I'm gonna up the payment amount to a thousand dollars. I'll text the address to you. Keep this shit between the two of us, my nigga. I don't need nobody knowing my moves."

"A'ight, text me the address and I'll be on my way."

I hung up the phone and texted him my location. Nova had been in the bathroom long enough, so I went to get her out of the tub. When I got to the door, she was standing in front of the mirror dressed in the shirt I gave her. The shirt covered up to her mid thighs and them joints were thicker than I remembered. I wanted to bend her fine ass over that sink, but I didn't think that would be a good idea right now. I felt my phone vibrate in my hand and I looked down to see that it was a text from Conte.

Conte: *I got the info and I'm on my way. I'll be there in about forty-five minutes.*

I didn't bother replying. I just needed her to eat, so I could bound her ass back to the bed. When I looked back at her, she was staring at me through the mirror. If looks could kill, I would be one dead muthafucka. I gave her body another glance and met her stare head on.

"Why are you looking at me like you are about to fuck me right here? I want you to know that it ain't happening. I don't give a fuck what you're thinking," she said, rolling her one good eye.

"Ain't nobody thinking about fucking you right now, but I am gonna get in them guts real soon, ma. Right now, though, I'm gonna need you to make your way back to the bed so you can eat. I'm not about to let you starve yourself on my watch. Let's go," I said, stepping aside so she could walk in front of me.

When she was in front of me, she shook her head while looking at me. "You don't want me to starve myself to death, but there's no hesitation when you are trying to beat me to death, huh? Such a fucking hypocrite, pussy ass." She mumbled that last part, but I heard it. I let it slide because I didn't feel like fighting with her.

She walked to the bed and looked at the sandwich. She lifted the bread and everything in between. She smelled it, then looked it over again. After examining the sandwich, she placed it back on the plate. This is what she'd been doing every time I brought her something to eat.

"Do you have some crackers? I'm not eating shit that you didn't prepare in my presence. You can take this back because I don't want it."

She lay in the bed and placed the cover between her legs and held her arms above her head. I guess she was ready for me to tape her back up. I wasn't about to argue with her ass. I did what she silently implied. As I bounded her arms, my phone started buzzing in my pocket. Whoever it was had to wait because I wasn't giving her the opportunity to fight her way out of here. I completed the task and pulled my phone out. It was Conte. Before I could dial him back, I heard the doorbell.

"Okay, I'm about to bust this move really quick. I don't want my nigga calling telling me that you in this bitch acting a damn fool. Do you hear what I'm saying?"

"I don't give a fuck what you are about to do. If it don't have anything to do with you letting me out of this mutha-fucka, then you don't have to inform me of the shit. Move around, nigga. Bye."

There she was talking slick at the mouth again. I didn't have time for that shit. I shook my head and went to answer the door.

Meesha

Chapter 9

Nova

When I say that this muthafucka made my ass itch, he *made* my ass itch. I was waiting on his punk ass to *try* to get some of my goodies. I would have bit his fucking dick off. I wish I would let his nasty ass fuck me, knowing he fucked with that hoe bag bitch Ziva. That bitch ran through niggas like the quarter hand on a clock. Then he had the nerve to talk to me like I was a child misbehaving or some shit. Nigga, I'm a grown ass woman. I don't need anybody to watch me. His ass was terrified I would get out of this bitch like a mouse caught in a trap. But I'm gonna be cool and chill. This shit is gonna come to an end sooner than later. And when it does, baby, muthafuckas better watch out.

Thanksgiving was three weeks away. I'm not trying to eat crackers and sandwiches for the holiday, bound to a fucking bed. Nope, that's not happening. I want to be in the presence of my girls and my man. I had been praying the entire time I've been here, but I don't think God is listening to me because every time I pray, I end up talking about how I was contemplating to kill these bitches. He wasn't trying to help me because he knew once I was free, I would be doing the devil's work.

The door to the basement opened and Kelvin and an unknown guy was descending the stairs. He had the nerve to bring some random nigga to so call watch over me. He better hope this muthafucka knew to keep his hands to himself. I didn't have a problem making my body count rise. I had never killed anyone in my life, never even thought about it. But when a muthafucka had been through the shit that I had, that shit kept running through your mind constantly. It was going to be detrimental for all parties involved, including the stupid nigga that agreed to *watch me.*

"Look, all you have to do is sit and make sure she don't try to get away. I will be back in a couple of hours. Under no circumstances are you to let her get up," Kelvin said to the guy.

"Nigga, what if she has to go to the bathroom? I'm not trying to sit in this muthafucka, smelling piss and shit until yo' ass get back. Why the fuck yo' ass got a damn female in this muthafucka tied to a bed anyway? This shit could bring all kinds of heat yo' way, my nigga. I don't want no parts of this shit."

The two of them finally walked into the area where I was being held and this nigga sounded like he was about to bail on Kelvin's ass.

"Man, shut the fuck up! This is some easy money and you don't even have to touch her. As a matter of fact, yo' ass bet not touch her at all. This is my bitch, nigga, so keep ya muthafuckin' hands to yo'self! Do I make myself clear?" Kelvin snarled.

"What the fuck I look like trying to take advantage of a female that ain't willing to give me the pussy? That's some sick shit you just implied. And how the fuck is that yo' bitch, but she bound to a muthafuckin' bed? Yo' ass sound stu—" The dude stopped talking mid-sentence. I looked at him when he walked into the light. I was smiling on the inside. This stupid nigga recruited a muthafucka that knew me to stand watch.

"What the fuck you lookin' at, nigga? You don't have to stare so hard at her. What? Yo' ass know her or something?"

Damn, my heart deflated because Conte was a straight up nigga and could never lie about anything. My chances of getting out of there had ended before it could get started.

92

"Naw, nigga. I don't know that bitch, but I can tell she is finer than a muthafucka despite the swollen eyes and bruised mouth. You did a number on her, fam, but yeah, she sexy than a muthafucka," he said, eyeing me lustfully.

I couldn't believe my luck. That nigga lied like a pro. Maybe life taught him how to get out of many situations by lying. I'm glad he found that craft because he didn't know how much I needed that lie to come out.

"This the shit I'm talkin' about! *Don't fuckin' touch her* and I mean that shit!" Kelvin yelled. "I'll be back in a couple hours. Take heed to what I said. I bet not come back and you done violated in anyway. I will shoot yo' ass between yo' muthafuckin eyes, nigga."

"A'ight, I heard you the first time, nigga. I got this. Gone 'head so you can get back to this messy shit that you got going on in this bitch," Conte said, sitting in a chair in the corner playing with his phone. "Oh, yeah. Let me get my money before you leave. This ain't no 'work to get paid for later job', nigga," he said, holding out his hand. Kelvin looked over at me and pulled a knot of money from his pocket. He counted out the bills and handed it to Conte. He walked up the stairs and out the door.

***

As soon as I heard Kelvin's car start up, I started asking Conte question after question.

"What are you doing here? How do you know Kelvin? Were you in on this shit?

"Sabrina, shut up and listen to me!

"My name is not Sabrina, it's Nova. Get that shit right! Now, answer my fuckin' question!"

"My bad, Nova. I did not know anything about this shit. He called me up to come sit with a female. I had no clue that

93

he had the woman held against her will. And I damn sure didn't know it was you. G is going crazy trying to find you. I'm the one that gave him all the information he needed about what happened at the club. I'm with you, ma, not against you. As a matter of fact, let me cut this shit off you."

He walked over to the bed and started cutting the tape from my arms and then my legs. Once I was freed, I looked around for my clothes, but I couldn't find them. I went to the closet while Conte went into the bathroom. I found a pair of jogging pants and some socks. I put the clothing on and spotted my tennis shoes in the corner. Picking up my shoes, I sat in the chair and started to put them on.

"Don't put those on just yet. Let me clean those wounds so they won't get infected. That muthafucka did a number on you, ma. He needs his ass whooped."

He started putting hydrogen peroxide on my wounds and that shit burned a little bit. He dried it off and applied triple antibiotic ointment, as well. He used gauze to wrap my wrist and ankles, holding it together with medical tape. I don't know how he found all that shit, but my limbs felt good for the moment. He then helped me put my shoes and socks on.

"Let's get the fuck up out of here before that nigga comes back. I'll hit Quan up when we get in the car."

"Why Quan? Why not Grant?" I asked.

"Quan's the only person that I have a number on, ma. If I had someone else's I would use it, but I don't," he explained.

When he said that, I started looking around praying that Kelvin's stupid ass left my phone in this muthafucka somewhere. I checked drawers, tabletops, closets and everything, but I didn't see my phone anywhere. I didn't want to chance getting caught trying to find a damn phone.

"What the hell are you looking for?" he asked as he watched me tear shit up.

"I'm looking for my fuckin' phone, but I don't see it. Let's get the fuck outta here. I'll get another phone. I guess Quan can get the word out to my baby."

We got upstairs and the house was beautiful. I was wondering how long he had this place while looking around. I didn't know anything about it. There were beautiful oakwood trimmings around the windows and doors throughout the house, big bay windows and nice furniture. As I was surveying the interior, I spotted my phone on the coffee table. I scooped it up and tried to power it on, but it was dead. I headed straight for the door with Conte right on my heels. I didn't want to look around anymore. I wanted to get home and soak comfortably in my own tub and cuddle up with Grant before I put this plan in motion to eliminate these bitch ass muthafuckas.

I practically ran out of that house, jumping into Conte's car. He got in on the driver side and didn't hesitate about getting out of dodge. He connected his phone to the bluetooth and dialed out. The phone rang several times then it was answered.

"What up, Conte? I was supposed to call you days ago, but I'm glad you called. I may need you to find out some information on that nigga, Kelvin. He kidnapped Nova and we need to find him before he does something bad to her. I'm gonna need you to get—" Conte cut him off before he could finish.

"Not to cut you off, but that's why I am calling. Kelvin called me to this spot in Itasca to watch a female while he went to take care of some shit. When I got there, Nova was bound to the bed. I acted like I didn't know her and played it off. Baby girl's right eye is swollen shut and he had her taped to a muthafuckin' bed! But to make a long story short, I got her Quan. Where do you want me to take her? Where is G?"

"That muthafucka! G is in Atlanta. He went down there with Scony because his grandma passed away last night. We have been all in these streets trying to find this nigga and Nova. I'm so glad that nigga was dumb enough to call a muthafucka that she knew. Meet me at GSpot, but don't let her get out of the car. I'll be there to scoop her up. Thank you for this, Conte man. I appreciate this shit for real."

"No problem. I'll be there in about an hour or less."

"A'ight. One," Q said, disconnecting the call.

I couldn't wait to get home. I was about to be passed off like a fuckin' drug deal. I had to go all the way from Itasca to Downtown, then all the way to Country Club Hills. I just wanted to relax and go to sleep, but I would be cruising around for however long. But it was better than being taped to that got damn bed.

***

I was so sleepy, but I refused to close my eyes. Even though Conte rescued me from Kelvin, I didn't trust myself to let down my guard. I had been wondering how Kelvin was so comfortable calling him up. It wasn't sitting well with me. He may be an expert at lying now. Shit, I didn't know. I hadn't seen Conte in years since he left the hood and moved to Indiana. But now I see him for the first time and he was affiliated with this crazy bastard in some type of way. I decided to stop speculating and just question this nigga.

"Conte, we go way back and I have never had any problems with you. In fact, you treated me like family back in the day, so I need to know how you know Kelvin?" I asked, turning my head to look at him.

He reached over to lower the radio and let out a long sigh. He didn't say anything for about a minute, and then he began to speak.

"I met Kelvin through this nigga named Sergio. They were close, but it was only because them muthafuckas was on some

96

shiesty shit, you feel me? I went to get my weed from Sergio and I would see that nigga Kels on occasions. But when that nigga didn't have any remorse about the shit he did to you, I lost all respect for his ass. I knew all about Sergio jackin' niggas, but I didn't know anything about Kels being a part of it until that shit went down on the Nine. When Sergio got to braggin' about how they ran through there killin' Scony's little cousin and praising Kels about shooting you, I had to fall back from them. It rubbed me the wrong way, but what threw me for a loop was when I heard Kels talking to Z. That's when I started putting everything together. I met up with G and told him everything that I knew. I ain't never been a snitch nigga, but that shit wasn't right at all. I couldn't keep that shit to myself. All of them muthafuckas need to be dealt with. I didn't know about them niggas coming to your crib either. I had nothing to do with none of that shit that they did. I was about to tell that nigga no when he called me this morning, but something kept pushing me to come and I'm glad I did." He glanced in my direction and continued to drive.

The shit Conte told me had me convinced that he didn't have anything to do with any of the things that went on these last couple of months. Maybe God was listening to me when I was talking to him because he surely answered my prayers about me getting out of that situation. Now he must forgive me for the blood I'm about to leave across the city limits.

Meesha

Chapter 10

Quan

It was just my luck when that nigga Conte hit my line. There was so much going on at once, I forgot to hit that nigga up, but he ended up hitting me with some good muthafuckin' news. I couldn't wait to tell G that I had Nova with me. I was going to wait until she was standing in front of me before I made that call, though. I should've had Conte put her on the phone so I could hear her voice for myself. But he had been on some real shit when it came to Kelvin so far, so I was going to give him the benefit of the doubt. I wasn't calling anyone just yet. I was thinking about how I was about to put in work on this mission. Yeah, I was just the brains in this organization, but I was about to get my hands dirty this time around. Kelvin had lost his damn mind doing all the shit he had done and the bitches weren't getting off scot-free either.

When I pulled up at GSpot, my nerves were all over the place. We had been trying to track this nigga down for weeks and going hard the last few of days looking for Nova. Now that she was safe, we didn't have to tread lightly with this nigga. He is going to wish that he never started fucking with her to begin with.

I looked up when I saw a car pull into the parking lot of the club. I couldn't remember if this was that nigga Conte or not. Whoever it was, pulled in next to me and my hand was massaging the trigger of my heat. The door opened and Conte stepped out and walked around his car to mine. I opened the door and got out with my tool still in my hand. I walked to the passenger side of his ride. I had to see if Nova was all right so I could call my nigga G with an update.

Snatching the door open, I looked in and Nova was sleeping with her head leaned back against the headrest. I shook her a little bit, but she didn't move. I saw her chest rise and fall with every breath that she took. Baby girl was out like a light. I leaned in to examine her face. When I tell you that both of her eyes were swollen, she looked like she went a couple of seconds in the ring with Mike Tyson. Her right eye was shut tight, her lip was big with a thick blood clot on the tip and her face was bruised up badly. I closed the door back and leaned against it.

"Conte, what the fuck happened to her face, my nigga?" I asked him with my arms crossed.

"I can't even begin to tell the you what the fuck happened to her. All I know is that I had to play that shit off when I saw her laying in that bed with her arms and legs taped to it. As soon as that muthafucka left, I cut her lose, cleaned up her wounds and hauled ass out of there. He's gonna be blowing my shit up once he notices we ain't there no mo', but I'm not worried about his punk ass. If I were strapped, I would have killed his ass myself. I will text you the address to the location he was holding her at and he has a new number. I will make sure you get all of that shit right now."

He took his phone out of his pocket and shot the information to my phone.

"He also said something about Ziva being out with Avah, so I think y'all gonna have to go after one of them bitches to get to his ass, real talk."

"Yep, they ass gonna get it for sho! Them hoes wanted to dance with the devil, now shit just got real hot for them, too. But let me get baby girl to the crib. I got to hit my nigga up and let him know what's been going on. Good lookin' out and watch ya'self. That nigga is about to be gunnin' for ya. Hit my line if you hear anything or if you need some assistance. You

100

are covered by us from this point on." I dapped him up and opened the door to get Nova out.

When I looked in, she was staring at me and quickly lowered her head. At that point, I knew she was ashamed of the way her face looked.

"Come on, Nova, so I can get you to the crib. I'm gonna call G and let him talk to you."

"Just take me home and I'll see him when I get there. I don't have my keys or my purse," she said, stepping out of Conte's car.

"He isn't at the crib, Nova. G went to Atlanta with Scony. His grandmother passed away last night. I'm gonna call him when we get in the car, ma," I explained to her.

I walked her to my ride, holding her by her arm. I made sure she was in before closing the door. When I got in, I started up the car and turned on the heat. She didn't have on a coat and it was cold. I had a windbreaker in the backseat I handed her to put on. As she put the jacket on, I pulled my phone out and dialed G up. He answered on the third ring.

"What up, Q. Any good news for me?"

"I do have some news. Do you want the good news or the bad news first?" I asked quietly.

"Man, ummmm, shit, give me the bad news first." He was breathing real hard into the phone.

"Nova was beaten badly, fam—" I didn't get further than that before G cut me off quick as fuck.

"Where is she, Q? Have you found her?" he yelled. The fear in his voice could be heard miles away. I knew that he was thinking the worst, so I had to calm him down.

"G! The good news is that I have Nova in my possession. Conte got her away from that nigga Kelvin, but I don't know where he is though. Nova don't have her keys to get in the crib, so I need to know where you want me to take her. I called you before I called Tonio."

"Tonio has a key to my house. He's been checking on Lady while I've been gone, but I don't want her to be alone. Take her to Mom Dukes' crib. She will be safe there until I get back. Put her on the phone. I need to talk to her."

I handed her the phone and pulled out of the parking lot.

"Hey, baby." She sounded so drained and tired.

"Are you all right? Tell me what happened, baby." G was talking so loud, but soft once he heard her voice. I could still hear what he was saying though. Nova started telling him what she had gone through while she was in the crib with Kelvin.

Listening to her tell G what happened made my blood boil. That bitch Ziva will get what's coming to her, as well. The shit Nova said that hoe did was foul as fuck. That bitch named Karma was gonna find her ass and give her what she deserves. The tone of Nova's voice was kind of scary. She didn't sound like the sweet girl I had heard about. She had a tone that was satanic as hell. All I heard was revenge and death in her voice. I looked over at Nova and she handed the phone back to me.

"Yeah," I said, placing the phone on speaker.

"Take her to my mom's crib. I don't have a date on when we will be back. We are trying to get shit taken care of down here. Everything will be finalized to bring Grandma Liz back to the Chi soon, at least that's what we are hoping." He sounded stressed out, but relieved at the same time.

"Grant, your mama don't even know me. Why can't I just go to Mo's house?" Nova said loudly. I put the phone on speaker, so she could hear his response.

"My Mom Dukes knows all about you, Future. Believe what I tell you, she is gonna welcome you with open arms. Do you trust me?" G asked.

"With everything in me," she responded without hesitation.

"Alright then. Do what I ask. Okay, baby? I'll see you soon. I love you, Nova LaCour."

"I love you, too, Grant," she said quietly.

"Aye, Q. Hit Tonio up and give him a rundown of everything that went down. Be ready to suit up when I get back. This muthafucka been running the streets too long. He better pray long and hard her face clears up before I get back in the city. I'm out," G said, disconnecting the line.

I put the phone between my legs and continued driving. We were on our way to Flossmoor so I could take Nova to G's mom's crib. Kelvin better stay low because that nigga's life was on a short timetable at this point.

Meesha

Chapter 11

G

Hearing Nova's voice had tears forming in my eyes. I was glad that she was all right and I was grateful that Conte was the one that went to that house for that muthafucka. But all that shit went out the window when she started telling me what he did to her. I was ready to fly back then, but my nigga needed me right now. I'm going to put a plan in motion as soon as I finish talking to my Mom Dukes about Nova. Grabbing my phone off my hip, I found her name and pressed it.

"Hey, baby. How is everything going?" she said when she answered.

"Everything is going according to plan here, Ma. Scony is going through it, but he is holding on strong. He really has to be the strength in the family now. He has to make sure his sisters are okay. We are bringing MaKayla and MaKenzie back with us. Scony don't want them down here alone."

"Aren't they twenty now? What do they want to do?" she asked.

"You know they are not gonna be grown in Scony's eyes for a very long time. I actually agree with his decision. The twins are gonna need guidance so they won't be out doing stupid shit—I mean stuff. Scony needs to be close enough to keep them in line, Ma, so they don't have a choice. But, Ma, that's not why I called. I need a favor. Quan is about to bring Nova there. Would you keep her there with you until I get back?"

"They found her? Praise God! I've been praying every time I thought about what was going on since you left. But you know you didn't have to ask me that silly mess!" she yelled with excitement in her voice.

Even though she had never laid eyes on Nova or talked to her for that matter, she knew how I felt about her.

"As much as you talk about that woman, expressing your love for her, telling me how strong she is and how you love her ambition. She is the one for you and if you love her, she will always be welcomed in my home. With or without you, both her and my grandchild will always be welcomed here. I'll keep an eye on her. As a matter of fact, don't worry about her. Hurry up and get your ass back here. That's what I need you to do. I love you, son. I'll text you when she gets here," she said excitedly.

"I love you back, Ma. I owe you big time."

"You don't owe me shit! Get off my phone, Grant." She had the nerve to hang up on me.

I smiled for the first time since Nova was snatched up. I felt like all the stress in my body was lifted. Now, to put the first part of my plan into motion, I scrolled through my phone, landing on the name that I had been avoiding for months. This was my ticket to Kelvin's ass and I'm about to cash out on it. I'll talk to Nova about it once the ball was in my court.

My finger lingered over the name for about five minutes. I didn't even want to press that bitch, but I knew that I had to. Fuck it, what will it hurt? I pressed the name and listened to the phone ring. When she was answered, I heard laughing in the background.

"Shhh, hello." This bitch was entertaining a muthafucka at my expense I see. I was about to show her ass why she was still chasing a nigga.

"Hey, what's up, Avah? You have been hitting me up for a minute, so I decided to hit you back."

"Oh, really? What made you decide to dial my phone now? Your bitch left that ass, huh? Or did you realize that I was the best choice for ya? Which one?"

This bitch was being real comical right now, but I had to keep my cool for my plan to work. I let all that smoke she was blowing go in one ear and out the other. But not before it passed through my brain and stayed there. I was about to respond, but I heard a female in the background. The shit she whispered made me close my mouth.

"His bitch may not be breathing right about now," she whispered and laughed.

"Hold on for a minute," Avah said, trying to cover the phone and mute the conversation.

"What the fuck you talking about, Ziva? I'm lost. You are laughing like that shit was an insider or something," Avah said.

"Don't worry about it. I didn't mean shit by it. Finish your call, boo, so we can get up out of here. I have something to do in a few."

I sat listening as Ziva shut Avah's ass down. They didn't need her stupid ass anymore and now this bitch is being the phony bitch that she was born to be. That let me know Avah didn't know what the fuck Kelvin and Ziva had done. But I was going to make sure her muthfuckin' ass found out whatever it was that I needed to know. I didn't give a fuck what she would have to do to get the information either.

"My bad. I'm back," Avah said with an attitude. I picked the conversation up where we left off.

"Look, Avah, I didn't call to talk about another bitch. I called to talk to you. I was wrong for putting my hands on you at the club. You were pushing major buttons that day. You puttin' yo' hands on me made me react, but I'll be man enough to apologize to you, ma. I wanna make it up to you. Can I take you out when I get back in town?" I put that shit on thick as hell, but I had more shit in my pocket if I had to throw it out there. But I knew that I had her thirsty ass right where I needed her.

Smacking her lips, she said, "I don't know, G. That shit was disrespectful as hell, but I'll think about it."

"Bitch, stop frontin' and go out with the nigga! Why the fuck is you trying to play hard to get? His ass is all you've been talking about, with his 'ain't shit' ass."

Listening to this bitch pop off like I was an average nigga, I chuckled. I couldn't wait to put two in that bitch head. She was talking all that shit now, but she would be begging for her life soon.

"Tell that hoe to mind her muthafuckin' business! She don't know shit about me! I don't know who the fuck she is, but tell her that she may want to check her tongue before she lose that muthafucka. I'm gonna let you go before I stoop to her level. I'm not a bitch nigga, so I won't be doing the back and forth shit. I'll hit you up as soon as I touch down, Avah." I hung up on her ass before she could respond.

So many scenes were running through my head, I had to take a couple of deep breaths before I got up and went in to the bathroom to drain the snake. I washed my hands and started the shower to relax my mind. I couldn't wait to get back home to my babies. Hearing Nova's voice put a smile and a frown on my face damn near at the same time. When she retold the story of what that bastard did to her, I almost cried. But I'm going to give his ass a chance to square up with a real nigga before I lay his ass down.

Stepping in the shower after disrobing, the water was hot just the way I liked it. The tears of happiness escaped my eyes without warning. Nova had me in such a vulnerable state. I had to get this shit in order because when I get back to the Chi, all this crying shit is going to be nonexistent. Now that I know she is safe, it's time to blow some shit up.

***

The shower was everything that my body needed. I felt like a new man. I found a pair of black jeans and a throwback Blackhawks jersey in my bag and laid them on the bed. I rubbed my body down with some Gucci Guilty lotion, applied some deodorant and brushed my hair. Putting on my fit and socks, I took my all black Gucci sneakers out of my luggage and put them on. I open the door to go downstairs and Scony was about to knock on the door. He was standing there with his fist raised.

"Damn, nigga. I was just coming up to see if you were gonna sleep all morning. Aunt Sarah told me to come get you. Breakfast is ready. I see yo' ass been up," he said, looking at me like he was about to talk shit.

"Yeah, I've been up for a good minute, brah. Come in. We may as well rap now since yo' ass is already in my business." I stepped back from the door about to sit down.

"Nah, nigga. We can talk after we eat. I may need a blunt for the shit you about to tell me. And you already know Aunt Sarah don't play about her muthafuckin' food. I'm not getting my ass beat behind you, nigga," he said, laughing turning around to go downstairs.

I shook my head at his back and followed his ass down the stairs. "Yo' ass still scared of Aunt Sarah, pussy ass nigga," I laughed, pushing his ass down the last couple of steps.

That little gesture took me back to when we were younger. One of us was always pushing the other down the stairs. We anticipated that shit every time now, but it took a lot of practice to perfect that shit.

"Yo' big head ass better *still* be scared, too. You are not too grown to get fucked up, Grant," Aunt Sarah said with her hand on her hip. She was standing in the doorway of the kitchen with a big ass spoon in her hand.

"Gone somewhere with that nonsense, woman. Ain't nobody trying to hear all that. You already know how I used to flip you back in the day," I said, laughing while taking a seat at the kitchen table.

We all got quiet for a couple minutes because everyone was waiting for Grandma Liz to say, *"Cut that shit out. It's too early in the got damn morning. Nah sit ya ass down so y'all can eat."*

But we will never hear that voice again. I pulled my phone out to listen to the last voicemail she left me a couple weeks ago just to hear her voice. I pressed play and held it to my ear.

"Hey, my cat-eyed baby. I haven't heard from you in a couple days. Call the ol' lady when your hoe ass gets some time. And tell Demarius I'm kicking his ass because he's been neglecting me right along witcha. I love y'all, baby. Talk to you soon."

I remember that day like it was yesterday. I was deep in Nova's guts when she called, but when I finished I bet I called her right back. I laughed after I listened to the message a second time. I've been doing that since I got the call from Scony telling me she had passed.

"Hey, you good, nigga?" Scony asked.

"Yeah, I was listening to the voicemail again. I miss that woman, man," I said with my head down.

"We ain't doing this today. We're about to eat and then y'all can go outside in the back and smoke them twigs," Aunt Sarah said, breaking up our moment.

We both bust out laughing because she always called it weed twigs instead of trees. She brought both of us a plate filled with salmon croquets, cheese eggs, grits, toast and southern turkey sausage. Aunt Sarah sat down with a bowl of fruit in front of her. Both me and Scony looked at her like she was out of her mind.

"Um, where is your food, Auntie?" Scony asked, putting his fork down.

She smacked her lips and picked up a piece of cantaloupe and popped it in her mouth. "I'm eating it," she said, reaching for a strawberry.

"Nah, you're gonna eat more than that today," he said, getting up. He went into the kitchen and put a little bit of everything on a plate and placed it in front of her.

"And you won't be able to get up until you give me a happy plate," he said, trying not to laugh.

Aunt Sarah started laughing and we joined in with her until we noticed her laughter had turned into a full-blown cry. We both got up and hugged her at the same time. This was going to be a hard one to get over, but we will be there for each other no matter what. Once she got that cry out, we sat back down and started eating again.

"Aye, something smells good up in here! I hope y'all saved some for us because we are starving like Marvin around this piece."

All eyes were trained on the entry to the dining room, even though we knew who was blessing us with their presence. But that's not why we were waiting though. We had a bone to pick with these two muthafuckas. In walked Scony's twin sisters, MaKayla and MaKenzie. These two hot heads thought not coming in this muthafucka last night was the thing to do, but nah, that's not how shit works.

They are twenty years old, but that ain't grown and they wouldn't even answer the fuckin' phone when we were blowing their shit up last night. With all the bullshit that's going on in Atlanta, Scony was on pins and needles. He refused to drive around trying to find them, so he said he was going to be ready when they showed their faces.

Makenzie came in first, stopping in front of Scony giving him a tight hug. MaKayla went straight to the stove, reaching to get a piece of sausage.

"If you don't get your ass out of that kitchen and go wash your muthafuckin' hands! You know better than that shit!" Aunt Sarah yelled.

MaKayla's hand dropped fast as hell and she froze in place. She knew not to try that shit because she wouldn't have made it in the kitchen if Grandma Liz were there. MaKayla turned to walk out of the kitchen and Scony stopped her in her tracks.

"Stay yo' ass right there!" He gently pushed MaKenzie off him and stood up. MaKayla and MaKenzie looked at him with the 'here we go' expression on their faces. He looked between the two of them, not saying anything.

"What is your problem, bro? You are always trying to yell at us, but I'm getting tired of that shit!" MaKenzie yelled.

"If you curse one mo' muthafuckin' time, I'm gonna fuck yo' ass up!" he said, giving her the look of death. I knew not to get in the middle of what was about to go down. When shit hit the fan with the three of them, it was like a WWE match. I'm ready to be the ref, it's about to get ugly.

Chapter 12
Scony

"I'm grown! Don't try to talk to me like you're my daddy! If you want to talk to somebody like that, have some fuckin' kids and do that shit! Better yet, talk to the bitch that you had screenin' yo' muthafuckin' calls yesterday like that, but you better watch how the fuck you talk to me!"

I love my sisters, but I think I fucked up when I taught them to be tough and don't take shit from nobody, but I wasn't the nobody that I referenced. Listening to MaKenzie talk that tough shit, I had to laugh to myself because she was me in a skirt and the shit was kind of scary.

"Kenzie, you better watch yo' mouth and that's the last time I'm gonna tell you. Why didn't either one of you answer y'all phones last night? I was worried about both of y'all. The least y'all could have done was called and let somebody know that y'all was okay," I said calmly.

"You don't' give a fuck about nobody but yo'self, Demarius! When was the last time you came down here? You called and sent money like that was supposed to make up for yo' absence. That's a great way to practice being a deadbeat nigga. It took for granny to pass away for yo' ass to show ya face. Get the fuck outta here with that bullshit. I'm not about to be checking in with yo' ass. We couldn't even get you to answer yo' own damn phone, but you want to question me." MaKenzie had the look of disgust on her face.

I couldn't say shit back at what she said. I had been going through a lot these past couple of months. With Malikhi getting killed, Lovely going through her addiction and trying to help G with business, as well as the shit with Nova, I didn't realize that I was neglecting my sisters. I sent money and

113

called often, but I should have been there. They didn't come to Malikhi's funeral because my granny wasn't up for traveling, so the twins stayed with her and didn't come either.

"Look, I know I haven't been down here in months and I'm sorry. I have a lot of shit on my plate right now. That is not an excuse and I know that saying I'm sorry is not gonna make it any better. I called granny every damn day and I could only go off what she told me and that was that she was all right. Now, if there was something else going on, one of y'all should've been hit me up to let me know. Don't stand here trying to read me like I said fuck y'all, because that's not what the fuck it was." I stood there waiting for one of them to respond.

"Fuck you, Demarius, or should I call you Scony? It really doesn't matter. I'm done with this shit." MaKenzie stormed up the stairs.

I looked at her and shook my head, rubbing my hand down my face. I turned to MaKayla and stared at her. "Okay, your turn. Get it all out now because this will be the only chance you will get to talk to me sideways."

"I'm not going to try to shit on you, brah, but I will defend my sister. She has a point. You have been missing in action for months. Granny has been acting differently, but she always said that she was fine. When we tried to go to her doctor appointments with her, she always told us that they were just routine visits and wouldn't allow us to go. You already know how she was, stuck in her ways. Like you, we had to take her word for what she said. Kenzie is hurting, brah. She was the one that found granny laying in the kitchen on the floor," MaKayla said with tears running down her face. "She feels that this is all her fault because her and granny had a disagreement the day before about Kenzie staying out until four in the morning. But I tried to tell her that it wasn't her fault. She won't listen to me."

I walked over to Makayla and wrapped my arms around her. She broke down and laid her head on my chest. These were my babies and they were hurting. I rubbed the top of her head, letting her cry.

"Kayla, everything is gonna be all right, baby girl. I'm sorry for not being here physically. I have something that I want to talk to you and Kenzie about later, but for now, get you something to eat," I said, kissing her on her forehead. I released her and she stood on her toes and kissed my chin.

"I love you, bro. I'm leaving when you leave. I won't be able to stay here after this. Granny was my everything and she's gone," she said, walking away towards the bathroom.

"Kayla," Aunt Sarah called out to her. She turned around waiting on what was to come next. "Tell Kenzie that I'm beating her ass for all that cursing she did in my mama's house."

We all laughed. I knew that shit was not going to end on that note without Aunt Sarah getting her input in. My food was cold as hell and I didn't have much of an appetite anymore. G already knew what I needed. I looked over at him and he had a bag of that fire in his hand waving it at me.

"Let's go out back, nigga. I got just what the doctor ordered," he said, getting up picking up his plate walking into the kitchen.

I followed right behind his ass, dumping the rest of the food in the garbage. I grabbed a bottle of water out of the refrigerator and walked out of the kitchen.

"Roll that shit up, G. That right there is about to get me right. That damn MaKenzie came at me hard as fuck," I said, laughing.

"Man, I'm gonna roll up when we get outside. You know damn well Grandma Liz didn't play that shit up in here. And Kenzie is you with a pussy, nigga. She gave you a run for yo' money. I told you a long time ago not to teach that girl all the shit you did. You better watch her ass. She got a slug with yo' name on it," he said, laughing walking pass me.

"That's what I'm afraid of. I would hate to have to shoot her ass back. We gon' be two dead muthafuckas, though," I said, laughing walking out the door.

***

It was nice as hell in Atlanta. The weather was seventy-five degrees. Compared to the cold that I left back home, this was the type of weather that I would run to. I hated the cold, but I couldn't see myself leaving my city for nothing in the world. Me and G was sitting on the patio. He was rolling blunts and I was in deep thought. The shit Kenzie said to me was lowkey fucking with me, but I will make it up to her, I had to. I was going to talk to them later on this evening about going back to Chicago with me. MaKayla already said she's rolling out when I do. I just had to get MaKenzie to not fight me on this. She was going if she wanted to go or not. She didn't have a choice in the matter.

My granny took us in when my mama passed away fifteen years ago from ovarian cancer. She did all that she could to take care of us, making sure that we focused on school and continued to do well. Trying to keep me out of the streets was one of her toughest battles. At the age of thirteen, losing the only person that I loved with my whole heart hurted like hell. It lead me to the streets, which helped me get my mind off her death. I didn't stray away from school because getting an education and my diploma was something granny didn't play about.

Seeing how we were struggling and granny working hard as hell to take care of me and my sisters didn't sit well with me. I got my ass beat often, grounded and finally she sent my ass to boot camp. She said that she wasn't going to sit back and watch me throw my life away. I wasn't mad at her at all. She did what she thought was best for me. But all of that shit didn't stop me because when I came back home at the age of nineteen, shit was the same as it was when I left. I got my high school diploma while I was away and she was proud of me.

I hooked up with G and we started getting money. When I would go home and try to hand my granny money, she would ask me where I got it from. I had to lie and tell her that I had a job. She didn't believe that shit at all, she wanted to see pay stubs. That wasn't a problem. All I did was have one of the many females that I was fucking with make me some. After that, she didn't question the money. I was smart with it because I wouldn't give her too much at a time, just enough so she wouldn't get suspicious. But whenever she needed anything, she got that shit.

It wasn't until one of her nosey ass friends went to her and said she saw me hanging with the local drug dealers. That was the day granny questioned me like she was the head nigga in charge down at the precinct. I denied that shit, lying through my teeth the entire time. Granny knew what the fuck it was. Her friend got all the juice in the streets and the shit was always on point. She put my ass out of her house, leaving me with some parting words that I carried with me until this day.

"Demarius, I'm gonna tell you this and then you can go live your life the way you see fit. The streets is a place that will eat you alive, but that's where you wanna be. I raised you to be a very good man, but you choose to be out there getting that fast money, I want you to be careful out there and know that I love you, but I won't watch you throw your life away.

Don't call me if you get locked up. I don't do jail for no damn body. Don't call me collect or don't ask me for money to come get your ass either. That's where them fools you hanging out with come in at. I have two other kids to take care of with my money. Take care of yourself. I can't have you dealing that shit and then coming to my house. All money ain't good money and I want no parts of it."

"Nigga, what are you over there thinking about?" G asked, handing me a blunt.

"I'm thinking about Grandma Liz and what she said to me years ago. I'm missing the hell out of her and I know that I have to stand up and take care of the twins, man. She didn't agree with what I do for a living, but she respected my hustle," I said, lighting the blunt.

"Yeah, I know how you feeling, but we will figure shit out and things will be all good, my nigga. Let me fill you in on what the fuck has been going on back at the crib. That nigga Conte came through. He got Nova back." He went on to tell me the story that was told to him and everything that Nova said when he talked to her.

"That nigga beat her up and had her tied to a fuckin' bed! He is one pussy muthafucka. I can't wait to get back. That nigga is gon' wish he was dead the minute he sees my fuckin' face! She will be cool at Mama Rissa's until we get back. Have you talked to that nigga Tonio yet?"

As soon as I asked the question, G's phone rang.

"This him right now," he said, looking down at his phone. "What up, cuz?" He placed the phone on the table and put it on speaker.

"I just wanted you to know that I just left Rissa's crib checking on sis. She's fucked up, cuz. That nigga did a number on her face. I told her that she needed to go to the hospital to make sure everything was all right with the baby, but she wants to wait until you get back. She said that he didn't violate her in *that* way and he only hit her in her face. I want you to know that she is not the same soft spoken person that I met months ago, my nigga. She has changed. Her demeanor is different."

"What do you mean, Tonio?" I asked, blowing smoke out of my nose.

"What up, Scon. It's like she is a totally different person. Maybe it's because of everything that she has been through with this nigga. I don't know, but baby girl has bossed the fuck up. The shit she was saying made a nigga cringe," he said, laughing. "When she catch up to them, it's lights out. That's all I have to say. I have one of the lil' goons sitting, watching the spot in Itasca waiting for that nigga to show up. He hasn't been back as of yet, but they are in position. I'm out here in these streets looking for that bitch Ziva."

"Why are you looking for her ass so hard? I want that nigga! That's my focus right now," G said, getting mad.

"That's the muthafucka that Nova put me on—" Tonio was cut off mid-sentence by G.

"Fuck you mean that's the muthafucka Nova put you on! When the fuck she start calling the shots around that muthafucka?" G yelled with a confused look on his face.

"Nigga, did you hear what I said when I told you she was not the same person she was? She told me that she was not worried about Kelvin because his day was coming. She wants Ziva on a silver platter, my nigga, alive. She said that shit with conviction and then she said if I refused, she would go find the hoe herself. I didn't want to give her any reason to leave that house, fam, so I agreed. How long are y'all gonna be gone? You gotta get ya ass back here and tame this beast they created."

"We are trying to wrap everything up. If things goes according to plan, we will touch down in a couple of days. Don't let Nova do shit, cuz. She's carrying my baby and her ass ain't about that life. Don't let shit happen to her, Tonio," G said in a stern but deadly voice.

"Shid, before all this shit happened she probably wasn't about that life, but shorty knee deep in this shit now. Maybe you should call her. Hearing your voice is probably what she needs. I don't think I can stop her from doing a damn thing. Her ass may try to kill me, but I'm out. My condolences to you, fam. Keep ya head up. You know we got you when you touch down, fam. Until then, I'll hold shit down here," Tonio replied.

"Thanks, man. I appreciate that shit. A'ight, take care of business. One," I said.

"Aye, cuz. Let me find out that Nova got yo' ass shook," G said, laughing.

"Fuck you, G! Yo' ass gonna come back being Beauty and she is gonna be the Beast, nigga. Now hurry yo' ass back."

G disconnected the call and held his head down, shaking his head. He sighed long and hard before he started to speak.

"Man, I hope this shit didn't change my baby too much. I understand her being beyond pissed, but I can't have her out there trying to be on no savage shit. I gotta find out everything that went down. Something set her off and I needed to know."

Chapter 13

Rissa

Grant calling my phone early in the morning meant that something was wrong. I knew what he did in the streets. I tried early on to stop him from pursuing his career in the drug game. There was no use continuing to repeat myself every damn day, so I left it alone and let him transform into the G that he was destined to be. I'm proud of the things my son had accpmplished. He didn't let money change him at all. I did worry about him every moment of the day, but don't get it twisted, I would suit up without hesitation and go out in the streets and get dirty with mine.

I was deep in the streets when I was younger and I'm not too naïve to know what's going on. That's where I met Grant's no good ass daddy. The difference from now and back then, these niggas don't give a fuck. So my ears were always to the streets and I knew more than my son thought I knew. When he came to my house crying about Nova, I already knew. I just wanted him to tell me. Under no circumstances did I agree with him killing Patricia. She didn't have anything to do with the bullshit that her son had done, but I knew the code of the streets and her son put her in the middle of that mess. His ass better think long and hard about coming for me in retaliation though. I'm not the average mama. I know how to protect myself and my son didn't have shit to do with it.

Grant loves this woman because I haven't met any of the women that he has had in life. The last time he brought a girl home, he was in high school and that was many years ago. He hasn't brought another one around since. The doorbell rang, interrupting my thoughts. I walked over to the monitor that

121

was mounted on the wall. I saw Quan and a young lady waiting for me to open the door. I made my way to the door and opened it, stepping to the side so they could enter.

"Hey, Mama Rissa. How are you?" Quan said, stepping through the door giving me a hug.

"I'm fine, baby. I see something has to happen for you to come see me, huh?" I said, laughing as I closed the door.

"It's not even like that, mama. You know I love you."

"Yeah, okay. Save that shit for somebody else because I don't believe it."

I looked over at Nova. She had her head held down. I guess she was ashamed of the bruises that were on her face.

"Hello, Miss Nova." I said.

"Hello, Miss Davenport." she said lowly. She never lifted her head, so I walked over to her and placed my finger under her chin and lift her head.

"I don't care what you have endured, always hold your head up and embrace whatever it is. You don't have anything to be ashamed of. That muthafucka fucked with the wrong one. Grant don't play that shit at all, so trust and believe me when I say his ass is gonna get what's due to his ass. And I'm not Miss Davenport, hun. Call me Rissa. I'm not that damn old. Now come on so you can sit down."

I led her to the living room and turned to Quan after she was seated. "Are you staying for a while or are you leaving?" I asked.

"I'm gonna head out. I have some shit—I mean some things I have to look into. But if you need me, just call," he said, kissing my cheek.

"I'm gonna let that lil slip up slide this time because I know you are angry right now. Be careful out there, Quan. Don't let this muthafucka catch y'all slippin'. Keep your eyes and ears open."

122

"You already know, mama. I'll talk to you later," he said, heading to the door.

I locked the door behind him and went back to living room. Nova was sitting there in this oversized windbreaker staring straight ahead. This woman was broken. I don't know what her state of mind was before this ordeal began, but I could look at her and tell that she's not the same.

"Miss Daven—I mean Rissa. Do you by chance have an iPhone charger? I need to charge my phone so I can call Grant," she asked, without looking my way.

I stood up and went to get my charger from the bedroom. When I came back and handed her the charger, her hands were shaking and she couldn't connect it to the phone. I sat down and pulled her into my chest. She let out a loud cry. It sounded like she had been holding it in for a long time. All I could do was rock her back and forth. I couldn't imagine the shit that she had been through, but she was about to get all of that shit off of her chest today. Holding anything in that's stressful could kill the strongest person. I wanted to cry with her, but one of us had to be strong. Handing her some Kleenex, I took her phone and plugged it up.

I sat back down and waited on her to get herself together. "Nova, we are going to talk this out between the two of us. If there is something that you don't want Grant to know, I promise I will let you tell him when you are ready. But whatever the two of us discuss today, will stay right here. But you have to talk about it, baby."

"Why are you being so nice to me? You don't even know me like that, but you welcomed me with opened arms," she asked in between sniffles.

"I may have never held a conversation with you, sweetie, but I know all about you. Grant speaks highly of you and he loves you. That man has never talked about a woman to me, let alone send them to my house. He must really care about you because no one knows where he nor I lay our heads at night. So the reason I'm being nice to you is because I like the person that has made my son's heart accept love. He told me that you are pregnant, Nova. You and my grandchild are now a part of my family. Until you decide to deceive me or my son, you will always have a place in my life. Now start from the beginning. Tell me what happened."

I sat there and listened to her tell me what happened between her and Kelvin without any interruptions. The things she told me pissed me off with every detail she shared with me. Everything was coming together and I was understanding why my son was so mad about the situation. When she told me what that Ziva girl said to her, I was ready to go out and kill that bitch myself. How could she call herself a friend when she was doing her dirty for years?

That's was when Nova's voice changed. It wasn't the voice of the broken woman that walked through my front door over an hour ago. I had to look at her to make sure Nova was still sitting next to me. I knew when I woman had been through a lot. I also knew when a woman was conjuring up a plan that was going to be vicious, as well. This woman had plans of killing these muthafuckas. She hadn't said it yet, but I already knew. I used to be that woman.

When she told me how she ended up getting away, she sat for about five minutes without saying anything. She didn't show any emotions on her face, so I just let her sit there. Finally, she spoke.

"Mama Rissa, I'm gonna kill them muthafuckas. I know that Grant won't let me partake in whatever he has planned, but I'm gonna move around his ass. Kelvin will never let me be happy with Grant. He will continue to come for me. I will not live my life in fear. If that means that I will spend the rest

124

off my life in jail, then that's what I would have to do. But I will not keep living my life looking over my shoulder because this nigga don't know how to let go. As far as Ziva, she's gonna remember every minute of dying. It's gonna be slow and painful. Would you please show me where I can take a nap? I need to go to sleep," she said, looking at me with the sweetest tone. I stared at her for a spell and stood up, leading her to the bedroom upstairs.

***

I showed Nova to the guest bedroom. I made sure it was ready when Grant told me that he needed me to keep an eye on her. Her story kept playing in my mind. It took me back to the day I was forced to killed Grant's daddy. It took me a very long time to come back from that evil place I lost myself in and I didn't want that for her. I was going to try to get her to let the guys handle this situation. I didn't know how it was going to pan out, but I was going to keep trying.

I went back downstairs to start cooking dinner. I had some pinto beans with turkey tails, candy yams, cornbread muffins and a strawberry cheesecake on the menu. I had to make sure that Nova ate well while she was carrying my grandbaby. I was mixing the cornbread when I heard a set of keys in the door. Grant wasn't in town, so it could only be one other person that was walking in my house and that was Antonio. When he rounded the corner and came into the kitchen, I had my Sig Sauer P238 aimed at his head.

"Hold on, Auntie! It's me!" he screamed.

His arms instantly went to the ceiling. I lowered my gun and stuck it back into my apron pocket and went back to mixing my cornbread. He didn't say shit for a spell, but I could hear him trying to catch his breath. I couldn't hold my laughter in any longer.

125

"That was not funny at all, Rissa! You could've shot me, man," he said, taking a seat on one of the stools I had in the kitchen.

"Stop coming to my shit without phoning first, E.T.," I said, while chuckling. "What are you doing here anyway?"

"I came to check on sis and to make sure y'all was good over here," he replied.

"Shit, you could've did that over the phone instead of coming all the way over here. She's upstairs sleeping anyway, so that was a waste of a trip," I said, looking over my shoulder at him.

"Is she all right, Auntie?"

"How about you ask me yourself," Nova said, sitting next to him.

He turned so that he could look directly at her and the veins were protruding out of his forehead. That was a sign that he was really mad.

"It's not as bad as it looks, Tonio. I will be okay," she said, holding her head down. But she lifted it right back up, giving him eye to eye contact. I smiled on the inside because she was taking my words in stride.

"I thought you were going to take a nap, Nova," I said to her.

"I tried, but then I heard Tonio down here. I'm lying. I thought he was Grant, so I got up to see him," she said, blushing.

"I may as well help you down here, Mama Rissa," she said, getting up going to the sink to wash her hands. As she was drying her hands on a paper towel, Antonio started talking to her again.

"I think I should take you to the hospital to get checked out, sis."

"I'm fine. I told you that it is not as bad as it looks. These bruises will heal in due time," she said, grabbing the potato peeler and started peeling the sweet potatoes. "All I know is that I'm killing them, Tonio. I know that y'all have been looking for these two dummies with no luck, but I want you to find Ziva and I want her alive. That kill is all mine. I know you are gonna tell Grant, but he can't stop what's gonna take place. As soon as you get that call, I want to be the next call you make, not Grant. Y'all can handle Kelvin, but leave the stupid bitch to me. I apologize for all the cursing, Mama Rissa, but sorry, not sorry," she said, continuing to complete the task at hand.

I couldn't even be mad at her, I already knew where her heart was at that moment. I was hoping and praying that this did not interfere with the relationship that she and Grant had. I had to figure out a way to change her mind about going out there commiting this violent act of revenge.

Meesha

Chapter 14

Kelvin

Cruising down Madison Street, I was blasting that "Friday on Elm Street" by Fabolous and Jadakiss. That shit go hard. I was trying to get my mind off Nova, but something didn't feel right. Conte was more so Sergio's dude than mine, but he never opened his mouth about none of the shit he knew we did. So, I don't know where this uneasy feeling was coming from. I picked up my phone and dialed his number to see how everything was going. His phone rang a couple of times before he answered.

"What's up, Kels?"

"Yo, how's things goin'?"

"Shit goin' cool. There's not much to do but sit here. I mean the bitch can't get up and run, if that's what you're worried about," he laughed.

"That's what I wanted to hear. She ain't trying to talk you out of letting her go, is she?" I asked.

"Nah, she ain't saying shit. She's the same way you left her ass. I'm not touching a muthafuckin' thing around here. How much longer will you be? Your couple of hours are up, nigga."

This nigga had the nerve to act like he was tired of being there. He better sit tight and don't move an inch.

"For a thousand dollars, yo' ass will sit there until I get back!" I barked.

"Yeah, a'ight. You better lower yo' voice. I'm doing yo' ass a favor. I'll leave this bitch and yo' muthafuckin' money right here, nigga! I don't know who the fuck you think you talking to," he spat back at me.

"Yo' ass is gon' stay right there until I return. That was the agreement! Conte my nigga, don't try to change shit now. I have shit that I need to take care of and I'm on it as we speak. I'm trying to get this money now. I will hit you up later," I said, hanging up on his punk ass.

I was on my way to meet up with this nigga named Joe. I had to go all the way to the Heights. He was taking a couple bricks, weed and pills off my hands. When Sergio was killed, I went to his crib and grabbed his money stash, as well as his half of the drugs from the job we pulled on that pussy nigga G. I knew I should have took that shit to his family, but fuck them. They didn't give a fuck about him. He didn't let they ass know how he was moving anyway. So they couldn't miss something they didn't know about.

I merged onto I-94 and put the pedal to the metal. I was on the Southside in a quick twenty minutes merging onto the Bishop Ford. That was one muthafuckin' trip that I wouldn't be making again. It takes too muthafuckin' long to get out there. I had to slow down and do the speed limit because the law will pull you over for going two miles over the limit. This was not the time for me to be getting pulled over. I was dirty as hell.

I had been driving for well over an hour and still had about twenty minutes to go. I pulled a black out of the box and lit it, that was gonna have to do until I got off that muthafucka. As I was about to turn the radio up, my phone rang. Checking the dash to see who it was, Ziva's name was displayed. I guess she was out of her feelings.

"What it do, Z?" I said when I answered.

"Where ya at?"

"None of yo' muthafuckin' business! Don't call me asking shit after you stormed yo' ass out the way that you did!" She got me fucked up. I'm gonna teach her ass to stop playing these childish ass games with me.

"Pipe that shit down, Kels. This is me you're talking to. Don't get it twisted. I don't know how many times I have to say this shit to you. I was asking because I was out with Avah having breakfast and she got a call from G. He is trying to get up with her, but the bitch was trying to play hard to get. I'm gonna try to talk her into meeting up with him so she can get some information out of his ass. I think he is just trying to fuck while he's waiting on his bitch to pop up. Speaking of her ass, where she at?" Ziva said a mouthful and the wheels were turning in my head.

"Where the fuck you think she at? She's at the crib!" I yelled.

"How is she at the house and it sounds like yo' ass in the muthafuckin' car?"

"I paid somebody to sit with her. I had to go get this money. It ain't gon' get itself, smart ass!" She was really getting on my nerves.

"Who the fuck do you trust like that to watch a woman that is tied to a muthafuckin' bed, Kels? Nobody! Why didn't you call me?"

"For your information, bitch, my nigga Conte is there with her. I trust that nigga with my life, so I'm all good. He ain't letting her ass go." I waited for her to say something like okay or good, but she came back with some other shit.

"Did you say Conte? Light-skinned, tall, drives a black Monte Carlo?

"Yeah, that's him. Wait a minute! How do you know Conte? Yo' hoe ass fucked him, didn't you?"

"That should be the least of your worries, lil' stupid dude! You paid a muthafucka that knows her to so call watch her! She is long gone by now, Kels! You fucked up!" She was screaming and panicking at the same time. She was blowing shit out of proportion.

"Calm yo' ass down, Z! That nigga don't know her! He looked me in my face and told me he didn't know her. Plus, I just got off the phone with his ass and he is still there doing what he was paid to do."

"The same way you looked Nova in the face and told her you loved her after beating her ass. That nigga grew up with us, so I know for a fact he knows her," she said, laughing. "I'm going to the house to see what I already know. She gone, boo. I'll call you back," she laughed and hung up.

As Ziva hung up, I realized that my exit was coming up. I had so much shit going through my head, I had to hop two lanes to avoid missing my exit. I picked my phone back up and hit Joe's line, letting him know that I was about to pull up.

"Talk to me," he said when he picked up.

"I'm around the corner. Have the shit ready because I have to be in and out."

"A'ight, cool," he said, hanging up.

I pulled up to the address that I had for him. It was a single level home with a big ass front yard. This nigga was standing on the porch with a duffle bag in his hand. I shook my head because I knew damn well he didn't think I was conducting this type of business in the open. I got out the car looking at him stupidly. He started coming down the stairs and I quickly stopped him in his tracks.

"Take that shit back in the crib, yo! Are you serious right now?" I said through clenched teeth. He turned to go back up the stairs while I went to the trunk. I grabbed both bags that I would need and slammed the trunk closed. I hurried to get inside his house. I had a few choice words for his ass.

"Man, I don't do shit like this on the street! That's a quick way to get locked the fuck up, my nigga! Don't ever do that stupid shit no mo'whether it's with me or the next nigga. That's not how you conduct business!" I said, pointing in his face.

"Damn, my bad. It won't happen again."

"I know the fuck it won't! Who else in this muthafucka?" I asked, looking around.

"Only my daughter. That's it," he said.

I took my tool out of waistband and motioned for him to give me a tour of the house. "I have to check for myself because I will not hesitate to light yo' ass up for being on bullshit," I said to his back.

I was checking out every room we entered until I was satisfied that he wasn't on shit. We went back to the kitchen and got down to business. I dropped the product on the table, letting him see everything that he asked for. I even had a little extra just in case he wanted that, too, which he did. I counted the money in the money machine to make sure all of it was there. He went to a safe and grabbed the money for the extra that he wanted and I counted that, too.

I concluded the transaction and didn't even say shit to that sloppy moving nigga and headed to my ride. I put the money in the secret compartment in my trunk and closed it. I jumped in my ride, cranked it up and peeled out. I was driving fast, trying to get back to Itasca. I couldn't believe this nigga Conte played me. I decided to call his ass to see how he was going to react to the line of questioning I had for his ass. When I called, he didn't answer. I tried three more times and the nigga didn't pick up one time.

"I'm gonna kill this muthafucka!" I screamed, banging on the steering wheel. I floored the gas doing well over ninety miles an hour trying to get to my destination.

Meesha

A Distinguished Thug Stole My Heart 2

Chapter 15

Ziva

Kelvin's parents should have gotten their asses kicked for whatever they did to him as a child. His ass wanted to be so damn smart, but instead he was dumb as fuck. All he had to do was tell me that he had something to do today. I would've stayed with the bitch. He was too worried about me killing her, so that's why he didn't say shit. He better be praying that Conte didn't cut her loose. I already know that is wishful thinking, though.

Nova bossed up right before our eyes. I saw it as it transpired. She was not the same person that I grew up with. He messed up her mental for real. I was praying for my damn self because I knew she had it out for me, too. The things that I told her only made her hate me even more. I was speeding my ass off on the expressway trying to get to Itasca. I had to weave in and out of traffic in order to get ahead of these slow driving people. It was late afternoon and I didn't look forward to sitting in rush hour traffic. I was on a mission and nothing was going to prevent me from getting to this house in a timely manner.

Using the steering wheel as a coping mechanism, I tapped away at it with my nails. The nervousness that I was enduring was on an all time high. The good thing about all of this was the fact that G was not in Chicago. Avah told me all about how he wanted to take her out to make up for how he treated her. She knew damned well she wanted to jump for joy, instead she tried to play hard to get. She would be fucking and sucking until her jaws locked up, if given the chance.

I knew he heard me in the background, but I wasn't worried because the nigga didn't know shit about me, but maybe he did. Monica and Jade probably spilled everything they knew about my ass. But it didn't matter because I changed my phone number and I got a new whip. I hadn't even been home, so they wouldn't know where to begin looking for me.

I signaled to get over because my exit was coming up and this stupid old man wouldn't let me over. I cut in front of his ass. I could see him screaming and turning red. I was getting off of this expressway by hook or crook because staying on was not an option. When I got off, I still had fifteen minutes before I made it to the house. All I was passing was trees, not one house in sight. This area was perfect for a scary movie. I just wanted to go in there to see if I was right about Conte getting Nova out there, then I was getting the hell out of dodge.

Making the right hand turn into the driveway, I saw a black car parked in front of the house. I let out a sigh of relief because that meant that Conte was still there. I pulled on the side of the car and got out. I took the key that Kels gave me out of my purse and climbed the stairs. I unlocked the door and went in, closing the door behind me.

Not bothering to turn on any lights, I made my way to the basement. The lights were on down there, so I knew that Conte still had the bitch tied up. When I got to the bottom of the stairs, an uneasy feeling came over me. Shaking it off, I went deeper into the basement. The bed was empty and there was no sign of Conte nor Nova. I walked to the bathroom and it was empty, as well. I took my phone out of my purse and damn near ran up the stairs. Tripping on the step, I banged my knee.

"Arrgh, shit!" I screamed, trying to put my weight on it so the pain could subside.

It hurt like hell, but I had to get out of that house. I continued up the steps slowly, limping the entire way. When I got to the top of the stairs, I hauled ass towards the door. All I could think about was getting out of Chicago. The Goon Squad was not to be fucked with. They were coming for us the minute the word got back that Nova was free and she would be leading them right back to this damn house.

My stride quickened and I was almost to the door when a figure stepped in front of me. My breath got caught in my throat because I didn't know anyone else was here.

"What's up, Ziva?" he said with a smirk on his face.

I searched my mind for some type of recognition, but it was blank. I didn't know this dude, but he knew me. On the inside I was scared, but I refused to let the fear stand out.

"Who the fuck are you and how the hell do you know my name?" I knew that wasn't the time to get jazzy at the lip, but I needed to know.

"I don't know your grimey ass per se, but I know a lot about you. You just identified yo'self. Maybe you should've used an alias. If you had, maybe you would be going about yo' muthafuckin' day right about now. Unfortunately, that's not an option," he said, laughing.

"What the fuck does that mean? I'm gonna walk out of here the same way I walked in, nigga. I don't know why the fuck you stepped to me anyway. You better get out of my face!"

"Sweetie, look here. Right now is not the time for you to get smart with a goon."

He said that shit with his eyebrow raised. My heart skipped a beat when he slid that subliminal message in there.

"I could've shot yo' ass when you walked in this bitch, but I let you go ahead and look for whoever you were searching for. You really should learn to watch your surroundings,

137

especially when you are up to no good. How long did you and that nigga Kels thought y'all could hide out? Shit, you muthafuckas had us playing a real life game of Tom and Jerry out here. I hate running in circles, baby, but you ran right into the trap and got caught. Let's ride out, ma. We have somewhere to be," he said, grabbing my arm.

Scared was an understatement. I was on the verge of crying, but I wouldn't show him that shit. Taking a couple of breaths, I looked at him and snatched my arm away. "I don't have no muthafuckin' where to be—"

Before the words could get completely out of my mouth, I had a cold piece of steel pressed against my forehead. I snapped my mouth closed with the quickness, my tongue feeling like it weighed a ton.

"What was that you were trying to say? I can't hear you, bitch. Come on, let me hear it. You had so much to say a minute ago. Repeat that shit so I can blow yo' muthafuckin' head off. Nevermind, it don't matter. Bring yo' ass on. It's time for you to take this walk of shame," he said getting behind me and nudging me in my back.

I heard what he said, but my feet wasn't cooperating at all. When he nudged me, I stumbled, hitting the entertainment stand that was to my left. My brain waves finally got my feet to communicate and move. We got outside and the sky went from being sunny before I went in the house, to gloomy and grey at that moment. It felt like I was moving in slow motion and apparently I was because he pushed me roughly in my back. I hurried to his car and stood at the passenger door, waiting for him to let me in.

"This will not be that kind of ride, baby girl. Yo' ass will be riding in the back, all the way in the back," he said, laughing.

"Aw, hell naw! I'm not getting in that muthafuckin' trunk, nigga!" I screamed and tried to run away, but I didn't get far at all. He grabbed a hand full of my hair and snatched me back.

"Ow! Please let my hair go." I could hear my hair being ripped from my scalp with every yank he applied to my hair.

"Did Nova have a choice in the matter when yo' ass did the same shit to her? I didn't think so," he said, dragging me to the trunk.

My eyes got big as saucers when he said that shit. I knew then that I was about to die. I didn't try to fight as he unlocked the trunk. I knew then that the Goon Squad knew more than we thought and I couldn't even warn Kelvin. The last thing I remembered was the trunk opening and the excruciating pain to the back of head. After that, everything went black.

Meesha

Chapter 16

Tonio

Boss man, fire you, expire you
Me die before you? You liar, you
Niggas is dead off the hits I approve
Shit, I got the Feds wearing riot suits
Y'all niggas don't listen'
Whether streets or in prison
When we find them we twist them
Niggas waking up missing
Y'all don't understand we want y'all all to hate it (it's murda)

I was riding around listening to Jay Z spit that fire on his "It's Murda" track. That's how the fuck I was feeling, trying to find these two idiots, Kelvin and Ziva. When I left Rissa's house, I didn't know how to digest the things that Nova said. She was in beast mode. I called G's ass and told him that he needed to get back to the Chi. I was anticipating tearing shit up with my niggas, but that woman was about to make us fight over a kill. My cousin had his hands full with this one because she was not taking no for an answer.

Gas ain't cheap and I had been driving around for hours like a muthafuckin' Uber driver. It had never taken me this long to find no damn body before. I know they don't have too many people to help they ass like this. It's worst than trying to find Waldo's blind ass in a crowd.

Pulling up to Nicky's Gyros, I didn't realize how hungry I was until I got there. I opened the door and I saw a nigga walking fast toward my shit. My hand automatically snatched my bitch off my hip, but I continued to get out like I didn't see his ass. He pulled his hat down looking around, I guess trying to see who would see what he was about to do. Nigga should've done a little bit of research before he came at me trying to do that stick up shit. When he got close, he pulled his tool.

"Run yo' muthafuckin' pockets, playa. I want everything from money to the keys to this pretty ass whip. Don't try to be a hero because I'll pop yo' ass and still get what the fuck I want. So let's just do this shit and then I'll let you walk where you going."

I chuckled at this lil' nigga, while shaking my head. I didn't give him the opportunity to react. I motioned like I was about to give him my shit out of my pocket and blasted that nigga right in the chest. I didn't give a fuck if it was still kind of light out. The nigga came for me right there, so I sent his ass to the dirt motel, right muthafuckin' there. I stepped right over his ass, hitting the key fob to lock my doors to my car and went inside the restaurant to pick up my food. When I came out, there was a small crowd gathered around his ass. I moved around their ass, got in my car and pulled off.

That's what's wrong with these young niggas. They don't know how to work for what the fuck they want. All they knew how to do was rob somebody and shoot innocent people aimlessly. I wasn't about to play with their ass. I had enough bullets for all that wanted to test a real nigga. I wasn't even remorseful about laying his ass down. Whoever taught his ass the game of taking what didn't belong to him, should've told him to be prepared for whatever happened.

I was pissed the fuck off. I took my leather coat off and snatched my phone off my hip. Before I could find Monica's name, it started ringing. I looked at the screen briefly and saw that it was one of the lil' goons. I hit the phone icon to connect the call.

"Talk to me, lil' homie," I said with a little aggression.

"Yo, man. You good over there?" he asked.

"Yeah, I'm good. I just had to take care of a lil' nigga that tried to take candy from a real one. His ass is laying low right now, so that shit is a done deal. What ya got for me, though?"

"I got the puppy from the pound. Where do you want me to drop it off?" he asked in code.

"Is it the female or the male?" I shot back.

"It's the bitch and she prettier than a muthafucka, too," he laughed.

"Take her ass to the Dungeon. I'm on my way. Beat me there," I said, disconnecting the call.

That was music to my muthafuckin ears. We finally had that bitch Ziva and her ass will have a lot of explaining to do. She wasn't gonna die just yet. She was gonna lead us to that bitch nigga before we dispose of her ass. I picked my phone back up and hit G up. The phone rang a couple of times and went into voicemail. I hung up and dialed Scony's number and his ass didn't answer either. Fuck it, I would try again later. I dialed Monica's number. That's when I remembered that I hadn't called to tell her that we had Nova back. It was now after six in the evening and she had been over Rissa's since this morning. Monica was about to chew my ass out. I took a deep breath when she picked up the phone.

"Hey, Tonio. How's everything with you today? Any news about Nova?" she asked.

"Hey, baby. I've been really busy today, so don't get mad at me when I tell you this. We got Nova back this morning. It just slipped my mind to call and tell you."

"Wait, hold up! Did you say you got Nova back? Where is she, Tonio? I need to see for myself!" she screamed.

"She is at G's mom's house. I'm sorry I didn't call to let you know before now. I've been out in these streets—"

143

"None of that matters, baby, as long as she's safe. That's all that matters. Does that mean that dumb and dumber is off the air?" Damn, these women are learning the game by the day. She talking in code better than some of these knuckle heads in the street.

"Nah, baby. They still have airtime for the time being. I was on my way to you, but I have to make an emergency detour, then I will be over to rub your booty," I said, laughing.

She didn't laugh with me. "Sex is the last thing that's on my mind, Tonio. I need to hear from my friend."

She was serious about that shit, so I had to make shit right. I needed to be balls deep in some pussy. If all that was standing in my way was Monica talking to Nova, then call me a magician because I was going to make it happen.

"She has her phone, so give her a call. If she doesn't answer or hasn't turned it on, call (708)555-5698. That's my aunt's cell number and if you don't get her with that number, dial (708) 555-6247. That's the number to the crib. Now, can I come over later to rub your booty?" I was praying that she said yes because a nigga's nut sack was full as fuck.

"Yes, baby. You can come over. Thank you for letting me know what was going on. I'm about to call Jade. She's is about to be so happy," she said cheerfully.

"Okay, baby. I'll call you later. If you decide to leave the house, call and let me know because we haven't found these fools yet. Be safe, baby, and I love you." I hurried up and hung up the phone because that last part wasn't supposed to come out of my mouth.

I was trying to take things slow, but she was everything I wanted in a woman and I was going to make sure I kept a smile on her face. She deserved to be loved and I'm the best man for the job. I feel good about my decision and I'm going to go all out for her. I turned the radio on and Jaheim's "Put That

144

Woman First" was playing. A smile instantly formed on my face.

**

Pulling up to the Dungeon, I killed the engine and sat there for a minute. I had to get my mind right because I knew if I didn't, I would shoot this bitch a million and two times. But she was going to sit in here until I got the okay to make her lose all of her senses forever. Taking my one hitta from the armrest, I pulled out my canister filled with the shit I called my storm chaser. I stuffed that muthafucka to capacity and lit it up, taking a deep pull. Letting the smoke fill my lungs, I felt my anger subside slowly, but it was going to take more than that to get me where I needed to be. The only thing I had on my mind was murder. I finished my medicine and tapped the hitta in the ashtray, then I was ready to go inside.

I stepped out of my whip and headed inside. Unlocking the door, I turned on the light and walked to the other side of the room. I flipped a switch to let the the garage-like door open and my young goon pulled his car right in. Flipping the switch to close the door, I started getting the shit that I needed together. I grabbed some rope and pulled a chair to the middle of the room. I was so ready to make this bitch wonder how long she had to breath.

"Pop that trunk, youngin'. Get that bitch out of there," I said, walking to the back of his trunk.

He hit the button on his fob and the trunk popped open. This bitch was laying there looking in my fucking face like she was Billy Badass. I reached down and snatched her ass up by her neck and dangled her there for a few. Putting her down on her feet, I let her go because I wanted her to try to be tough. But she just stood there with her head held down.

"Why are y'all doing this to me? I don't even know y'all!" she said, crying.

"Bitch, please. You know exactly what the fuck this is. Yo' ass wasn't crying when you and that nigga had the upper hand on my people," I said, stepping to her with my fist clenched.

"Who is your people? I don't even know you."

"I'm quite sure yo' ass already know why you are here, so let's stop with the bullshit. You muthafuckas put ya hands on my family and thought that shit was gonna be the end of it. Y'all was gonna kill her and run? Was that the plan? Whatever you two dummies thought didn't pan out. Now yo' ass is about to take one for the team. Get yo' ass over there and sit in that chair," I said, giving her a little push.

She was moving too slow for my liking, so I picked her ass up with one arm and carried her to the chair and slammed her ass down. I tied her arms to the chair first and then I bent down to start tying her legs. She swung her right leg and kicked me in the side of my head. Before I could stop myself, I punched that bitch in the mouth.

"Oh my God! I'm sorry. I didn't mean to kick you, I promise," she yelled out in pain.

"Bitch, you meant it and you did it. Try that shit again and you're gonna lose a limb," I said, tying the last of the rope around her leg.

I stood up and wrapped a piece of rope around her waist and around the chair a couple of times, tying it in a double knot. Once I had her secured to the chair, I walked towards the switch to the door.

"Let's get out of here. I'm tired of dealing with this bitch. I need to get as far away from her as I can before I do something that I regret."

146

The lil' homie jumped in his car to back out of the Dungeon. Rolling his window down, he looked over at Ziva.

"Yo, T. You aint gonna tape that bitch mouth shut, fam?" he asked, turning to me.

"Hell naw, I'm gonna let her ass holla until she pass out. Can't nobody hear her ass no way. Every wall in this muthafucka is sound proof, so I'm not worried about that shit."

He laughed and threw me a head nod, backing out. I let the door down and walked to the door. When I reached to grabbed the knob, she opened her mouth to speak.

"I hope he kills all of you muthafuckas!" she screamed.

I turned around and said, "That will never happen. He's a pussy ass nigga." And I walked out leaving her ass tied up in that chair in the dark.

Meesha

Chapter 17

G

Scony and I had been in Atlanta for three days, trying to get Grandma Liz's remains back to the Chicago. We finally got the approval this morning, but we had to get in contact with a funeral home so that they can arrange the transport. We will then have to wait for them to make it here to Atlanta. They had to do the embalming before we could even think about leaving, so Scony and I was going to look up some funeral homes to get that shit going today.

We were almost finished packing up the house, Scony put it up for sale yesterday. MaKenzie was still pissed off at him, so they hadn't said two words to each other, but that shit stops today. Life was too short for this silent treatment bull. She found every reason to be outside this house. She was there now, so there wasn't a better time to send his ass in there.

I walked into Grandma Liz's room and found Scony going through some papers. I stood there for a minute and walked in, taking a seat on the bed. He didn't even look up or even address me, so I knew whatever he was reading had his undivided attention. He finally looked up with tears threatening to fall from his eyes. He blinked several times and they rolled down his face.

"What do you have there, bro?" I asked.

"It's a letter that granny wrote, man. She knew, G, and she didn't say anything," he said, handing me the letter.

I looked down at the paper and started reading it silently.

"Read it out loud, bro. I didn't finish reading."

I looked at him and I could tell that he couldn't *read* it himself and he was pleading with me to do the honors for him. Clearing my throat, I started reading the letter to him.

"Whoever is reading this letter only got the opportunity because the Lord called me home. That would be the only way your ass would be going through my shit!"

We both started laughing.

"I'm sorry for not telling any of you that I was sick. I didn't want any of you to stop living your lives to take care of me. My heart has been getting weaker as the days went by. I refused the surgery every time it was brought up by the doctors. Demarius, I hear you saying, "Why Granny?" I'll tell you why, baby. I didn't want nobody cutting on me. I lived eighty-four great years. I raised y'all to be strong and independent because I knew I wouldn't be around forever. I was ready for whatever the Lord had in store for me, My story was already written. I was just playing it out. Through it all, my babies were still my top priority.

For years, I made sure to pay my insurance premimium every month. There is an envelope in the very box your nosey ass found this letter. This is going to ensure me that you all will be all right in my absence. Demarius, I need you to do something for me, baby, Take care of Lovely. She was fighting hard to stay off the drugs, but it's stronger than her. Don't be mad at her. I want you to just love and support her.

Tell my angels, MaKayla and MaKenzie, to behave themselves and go back to Chicago with you. That's the only way they are gonna get anything that I left behind. Grant, I know you didn't think I was going to forget about my bright-eyed baby. Stay out of trouble, baby, and give that woman of yours all the love that I know you can give her. She is the right one for you. I can tell by the way you speak about her. Throw in your playa card and do right by her. Continue to be there for Demarius. I don't have to tell you to do that because that's comes naturally. I love you, my G baby.

Sarah baby, I love you. I know you're angry because I put on a front, but baby I didn't lie one time when I said I was fine. I was fine with whatever happened, so don't beat yourself up behind this. Make sure Demarius follow my wishes. I don't want a funeral! I don't want none of those fake ass people looking down at me with that fake crying. Have a memorial instead.

I love y'all, but I don't want yall to cry for me. I lived, I loved and I moved on with the Lord. Now it's time for me to protect you all at once. I'll always be by y'all side. With all of that being said, don't forget me because I will never forget you all.

Love always,
Grandma Liz

When I finished reading, I couldn't even lift my head up. It felt like I had been punched in the chest. I sighed and looked at Scony. He was silently crying, but he cleaned his face and smiled.

"I can't even be mad at her. She always called the shots around these parts," he said, shifting through the box.

He pulled out a couple documents and started reading again.

"Granny got everything planned out, brah. She got her obituary already written out. All that has to be done is filling the date in. The burial plot and the headstone is paid for in full. I will look at the insurance policy later. I am not interested in knowing how much money she left behind. I'm gonna continue to take care of my sisters like I've been doing. I need to go talk to Lovely. The shit Granny said is mind boggling. She knew that she was back on that shit."

"Nah, fam. You need to go talk to MaKenzie. She is the one that needs your attention right now. That shit with Lovely can wait. We will deal with that when we get back home."

As soon as I finished what I said, my phone started ringing.

"I have to take this call. It's Nova," I said, getting up to walk out of the door. "Go talk to Kenzie," I said walking out.

I walked to the guest bedroom and closed the door, answering the phone as I sat down. I put it on speaker.

"Hey, My Future. How are you doing?" I asked with a smile on my face.

"Hey, baby. I'm fine. When are you coming back and how is Scony?"

"He's hanging in there. This is hard on him, but we will get through this. Hang up so I can call you on FaceTime. We are getting shit in order as we speak. It may be a couple more days before I get back baby."

"Grant, I don't want you to see my face, so I don't think calling on video is a good idea. I need to talk to you about something that is very important to me. Baby, I need you to let me do what I need to do when y'all find Kelvin and Ziva. As a matter of fact, I'll let you guys deal with him, I just want her."

"Nova, you are carrying my baby and I will not allow you to bring any kind of harm her way. So that will be a no for me. I'm not about to condone that bullshit you talking right now." She was pissing me off asking me to allow some stupid shit like that.

"Well, I'm telling you now that I did the right thing and came to you about this situation. I see that you don't understand why I need to have a hand in this, so I am no longer asking for your permission. I'm telling you at this time that I'm killing that bitch and there is nothing that you will be able to do about it. You wasn't there when that bitch told me how foul she was being to me right under my nose for years! You don't know how it made me feel to know that she had a hand in my parents dying. So if that means that I have to go out in the streets of Chicago and find this hoe myself, then that's what the fuck I will do! But you will not try to keep me in a box locked away from these muthafuckas. They have beat me down for the last muthafuckin' time and they will pay for it!" she screamed.

The way she was talking had me stuck with my mouth opened. I knew that she had been through hell and back, but for her to talk to me in the tone that she did was not gonna happen. I'm not the enemy. I have been by her side through it all, so she better check her tone and realize who the fuck she was talking to.

"Nova, who the fuck do you think you're talking to? I'm not that bitch ass nigga that put you through all of this shit! I am yo' man and I'm the one that's supposed to protect you. That's my job! I let them muthafuckas get close to you because I wasn't there. I failed at being your man, baby! Let me handle this shit!"

"You didn't fail at anything! That muthafucka got close to me because of a jealous ass hoe! That's how he got to me! That didn't have shit to do with you. It was gonna happen if you were with me or not! Stop blaming yourself because it wasn't you! But there isn't anything that you can say or do to keep me off that ass. I'm killing that bitch as soon as I lay eyes on her." With that, she hung up. I tried calling her repeatedly and she didn't answer, so I gave up. Throwing my phone on the bed, there was a knock on the door.

"Come in," I said.

153

MaKayla walked in the room and closed the door. She sat in the chair across from the bed and stared at me. I didn't know what the hell she came in to say, so I just sat there and waited.

"I didn't mean to listen in on your conversation, but what I heard got me mad as hell. You mean to tell me that a muthafucka did your girl dirty and you won't let her get with they ass? What type of shit is that, G? You can't take this away from her, brah. Let her do what she feel she needs to do," she said, standing up.

"If you heard all of that, then yo' ass also heard that she is pregnant than a muthafucka, too. She is not about to put my baby girl in harms way! I don't give a fuck what you or the next muthafucka says, it ain't happening, Kay! Now that's all I have to say about this shit. She is not about to be out in these streets killin' no damn body! That's what the fuck I'm there for." I stood up, looking down on her little ass, but she wasn't backing down.

"I still say you are wrong for that shit! Them muthafuckas did her wrong as fuck, G! They have to pay for that shit and you know it. I know you are worried about your seed, but she need to do this herself. If that's what she wants to do, don't deprive her of that. Them muthafuckas deserve everthing that's coming their way, but I'm going to Chicago and I'm all in. You already know that I'm standing ten toes down. I don't know Nova, but I'm gonna get to know her as soon as I touch down." She got up and went to the door. As she reached for the door knob, I said one last thing to her.

"I don't want no shit from y'all in Chicago, MaKayla. Let us handle this. I don't need nothing happening to y'all because of the things that we are into."

"You and my brother should've thought about that shit before y'all taught us how to kill. Now it's time for us to show y'all what the fuck y'all trained us to do. I'm not trying to hear none of that bullshit you spitting right now," she said, walking out the door.

I sat back on the bed and couldn't do anything but shake my head. Once the twins set their minds to do something, there was no talking them out of it. I hated the fact that MaKayla heard my conversation. This shit was not gonna be good for them muthafuckas back home.

***

I thought about the things that Nova said and how she hung up on me. Tonio was on to something. My future didn't sound like the person that I fell in love with. With the shit that she had been through, how did I expect her to come out of that shit the same woman that endured so much pain and deceit because of them stupid muthafuckas? I couldn't, but I did expect her to respect the fact that I didn't want her out there on no savage shit. She ain't even about that life.

A little practice shooting a gun don't make no damn body a killer. She better sit her monkey ass down somewhere and enjoy being barefoot and pregnant. But for now, I needed to patch this shit up and put a smile on her face. I grabbed my phone and searched the internet. I didn't even know what the hell I was looking for. It would come to me when I got to it, I guess.

I lucked up and found this site called *Le Fleur Bouquets*. They sell flowers that last for a year. It was time for me to shower my baby with as many flowers as I could. The saying was to give the ones you love flowers while they were alive and that's exactly what I was going to do. I checked the site out and I loved what I saw. I ordered her five dozen of roses in five different colors, all in heart shaped boxes. I also ordered her a diamond Pandora bracelet with two charms that were surrounded in diamonds, as well. One charm was of a baby carriage and the other was a love note that I had engraved to say, 'My Future, I love u'.

I hope that will make her forgive me because all that shit cost a grip. Money wasn't an issue, but I needed her to still love me when I got home. I had finished submitting my order when I heard a loud commotion somewhere in the house. Making sure that everything went through, I rushed out of the room. I followed the loud voices and ran down the stairs. When I made it to the livingroom, the furniture was moved and there was nothing but space and opportunity for a muthafucka to scrap it out. I looked around and MaKenzie was squared up with Scony. He stood looking at her with a look on his face that said "pull it".

MaKayla was in the middle, trying to get them to stop whatever was about to go on, but neither one of them was listening.

Aunt Sarah was screaming at the top of her lungs, telling them to cut it out, but I already knew that nothing was going to stop what was about to go down in the middle of Grandma Liz's livingroom.

Chapter 18

Scony

When G left out of the room, I decided to put all of the documents that I found in my suitcase. I had read enough and I was in my feelings, so I wanted to go talk to MaKenzie and have a heart to heart with my lil' sister. Walking down the hall to Makenzie's room, I heard the music playing. She was bumpin' "I Don't Fuck With You" by Big Sean. I knew right then that she was still mad as fuck, but I knocked anyway. She didn't answer, so I banged a little harder and she still didn't respond. So the next thing I did was walked in that bitch. What did I do that shit for?

She turned around and walked over to her iHome speaker and turned the volume down. She had on a pair of leggings with a shirt that showed off her toned stomach with a pair of socks on.

"What the fuck is your problem, walking in my shit like you was invited? Respect my muthafuckin' space, Demarius! Now get out!" she screamed, turning the music back on. The song must've been on repeat because it started over. She went back to cleaning out her closet.

I walked over to the speaker and turned that shit off and sat on the end of her bed.

"Kenzie, I'm sorry that I wasn't here, sis. You can't blame me for this shit, man. We are better than this. I found a letter that Granny left and she didn't tell nobody about this shit. Didn't nobody know, but you want to blame me!

"If your punk ass would've been around, you would have known that something was wrong! But you were too busy in the streets of Chicago worrying about self! What happened to family first, nigga?" she screamed at me.

I loooked at her funny as fuck. I always put family first. That's how the fuck she was rockin' the latest gear of any brand and that's how her ass was driving around in a muthafuckin' BMW. This lil' girl was out of her fuckin' mind.

"Kenzie, I'm the fuckin' reason you flossin' the way that you are. I sent money to this bitch faithfully for all of y'all and this is the thanks that I get? I have a life too you know, but for you to be standing there blaming me for something that was in God's hands is pissing me off!" She hit a fuckin' nerve. I didn't mean to go off on her like that, but it had to be done. I wasn't about to take the blame for this one.

"You think you was doing something, brah? I had niggas taking care of me. I didn't come up off shit you sent this way. I took care of my muthafuckin' self. I didn't need your ass and I don't need you now," she said, putting her gym shoes on.

She stood tall, looking at me without blinking. "Fuck you, Scony! I wish it was your ass that died instead of my Granny. She deserves to be here more than your stupid ass."

She raced out of the door and down the stairs. I was right behind her ass like white on rice. She wasn't about to be wishing death on my ass and think she was going to get away with it. When she reached the bottom step, I grabbed her by her arm and turned her to face me.

"You are not about to walk out of here. We are about to talk about everything you want to get off yo' muthafuckin' chest now!" I said, looking down on her.

"Nigga, if you don't get the fuck outta my face, I'll fuck you up!" she screamed.

"I'm not getting out of shit until you talk to me. This is not how this shit about to play out. We have never not talked, we ain't about to start now." She looked down at my hand and snatched away from me. I yoked her ass up by the arm once again. That's when all hell broke lose.

Snatching her arm from my grasp once again, she stepped back and hauled off and punched the shit out of me. I held my lip in between my teeth because I had to remember that this was my lil' sister that was standing in front of me. I guess she took that gesture as me trying not to hit her. She started pushing furniture in every direction of the living room until there was nothing but space in that muthafucka.

"You wanna hit me, Scony?" she said, dragging the syllables in my name.

All I could do was look at her and shake my head. Then she opened her mouth and said the most disrespectful shit you could say to a man.

"That's what I thought, you pussy ass bitch!"

Before I had a chance to think about it, I had my hand around her muthafuckin' neck. She wanted to be tough, I was about to see how much she learned from me. I was going to give her the opportunity to showcase her skills.

"Y'all need to stop that shit, Scony! Let her go! That's your damn sister!" Aunt Sarah was screaming.

I wasn't trying to hear none of that shit. Kenzie muthafuckin' ass was wrong for that shit she let come out her mouth. I'm not one of these niggas she been fuckin' with, so she was going to learn today that I wasn't a fuck nigga. Shit, she should've known that shit already.

"If yo' muthafuckin' ass don't let me the fuck go, we are gonna have a problem in this bitch! I'm not one of them punk niggas that is scared of yo' ass! You trained the right bitch when you trained me. I'm not scared of you by far, so if this is what you wanna do, let's do this shit," she said through clenched teeth, getting out of my grip.

She stepped back and got in the boxer stance. She was ready for whatever the fuck I was about to throw at her. MaKayla stepped back in between us.

"Y'all aint about to do this shit! We are family. Kenzie, you need to check ya'self, sis. This is your muthafuckin' brother, yo!" she screamed at her.

MaKenzie pushed her out the way and swung on me. I dodged that shit and pushed her ass back. "You're gonna have to come better than that youngin'. You must've forgot that I'm a muthafuckin man. You won't win."

"What the fuck that mean? You being a man don't mean shit to me," she said, hitting me with a two piece. I felt the blood fill my mouth and that pissed me off. I reached out and smacked the shit out of her. I couldn't bring myself to punch her. She was still my sister.

"Now you done fucked up, nigga," she said, charging me. She kicked me in my nuts and I buckled, then she punched me repeatedly in my head. I had to put my arms over my head because the blows that she was throwing were haymakers. Her ass punched like a dude. I almost forgot who the fuck I was trying not to fight.

I found my footing and I reached back and and punched the shit out of her. She stumbled back and before I could raise my hand to knock the shit out of her again, she had her bitch aimed at my head. I wasn't afraid of dying, but I'd be damned if I died by the hands of my own sister. She had that muthafuckin' gun concealed good as hell because the clothes she had on shouldn't have been able to hide it.

"Kenzie, put that shit down! You are not about to do this shit! Put the gun down, ma." G said, stepping in front of her. I don't know when that nigga came downstairs, but at that point I was glad he did.

"He put his muthafuckin' hands on me, G. He was the one that told me that I was never supposed to let a nigga put his hands on me. Then he turned around and did the very thing that he taught me not to accept! Move the fuck out of the way. I have a bullet for this nigga, brother or not! Yo' ass can get one too if you don't move the fuck out of the way!" she said with tears running down her eyes.

I looked into her eyes and walked around G. I reached for the gun and she backed up.

"Stay the hell away from me. I don't want to shoot you, but I will."

I started to walk towards her again and I reached out to grab the gun. She didn't resist and I snatched it out of her hand and hugged her tight.

"I love you, Kenzie, and I'm sorry for not being here, but I'm here now. There is nothing in this world that will turn us against one another. We all we got and I'm gonna make sure that we are good as I always have. Do you love me, Angel? I will always love you, regardless of what we go through."

"I love you, bro," she said, crying in my chest. I handed the gun to G and he took it, shaking his head.

"You muthafuckas are crazy. I don't want to see this shit no mo'. We family around this muthafucka. Save that shit for the niggas in the streets. This ain't how we rock.

"So, was that your way of saying we can tear shit up when we get to Chicago?" MaKayla asked on the sly.

"Hell nawl!" Me and G screamed at the same time. She walked over to me and joined in on the hug that me and Kenzie still had going on.

We stayed in that position for a good ten minutes before I broke the hug. I looked down at both of them and told them to go finished packing. Both of them headed upstairs and Aunt Sarah stood with her arms folded over her chest.

"Go ahead and say what you have to say, Aunt Sarah," I said, staring at her.

"Why the hell you hit that girl like that? That's your damn sister!"

"Did you not see how the fuck she knocked the shit out of me? She better be lucky that's all I did to her ass. She hit like a fuckin' man!"

"Well, I'm glad y'all let that shit go. I was gonna be the one shooting both of you simple-minded muthafuckas," she said, walking up the stairs.

I turned to G and started laughing. "She hit me hard as hell, my nigga. I had to play that shit off. What the fuck was Kay talking about?"

Shit, I thought his ass missed that shit. I had to tell him even though I didn't want to.

"She heard me on the phone talking to Nova about her not catching a body. She read my ass, telling me that I was wrong for not letting her take care of Ziva and Kelvin herself. She basically told me that it was going down when we got to the Chi, my nigga."

"Damn, my granny would beat my ass if they got caught up in some shit. I will have to have a talk with her ass before she spit that shit in MaKayla's ear. I'll figure it out. Right now, I have to get this house packed up. Everything is a go with the arrangements. We will be heading home in two days."

At that moment, Scony's phone rang. He reached to pull it off his hip and hit the phone icon to answer it.

"Hello," he said into the phone. He was listening to whomever it was on the other end without saying anything. He then thanked the caller and looked at me.

"That was the morgue saying that the body was ready for release. I have to call the funeral home to make these arrangements." I went upstairs to grab the paperwork and called up the funeral home that Grandma Liz had listed in the documents. I gave them all the information they would need, as well as the cemetery information. I was told that that they would be in Atlanta tomorrow to do the embalmimg. We would be able to leave out on Wednesday. I also scheduled the memorial for Friday and we would be burying her the same day.

Meesha

Chapter 19

Monica

When Tonio called me and said they found Nova, I started twerking through the house. I was so happy that my sister was found. I went from screaming to crying in two point five seconds. I ran to the bedroom and grabbed my phone off the endstand and dialed her number. She picked up on the third ring and I couldn't stop the ugly cry that escaped my lips.

"Oh my God! You are okay!" I screamed into the phone. Hearing her voice was like music to my ears. Even though it had only been a short time, it felt like forever. "Them muthafuckas didn't hurt you, did they? Where are you? I'm on my way bitch!" I screamed.

All I heard on the other end was her laughing at me. I knew I sounded funny as fuck, but I didn't care. I walked into the bathroom to grab some tissue. I was looking like Lil' Roscoe from the show, *Martin*. I blew my nose and it sounded like a train horn and this muthafucka started laughing hard as hell. In turn, I started laughing right along with her.

"No, Mo, they didn't hurt me. The only thing they did was pissed me off," she said in between laughs. "I promise you that I'm all right, boo. I'm at G's mom's house in Flossmoor and I'm gonna need you to come get me right now! I'm tired of being in this house. On top of that, I got some shopping to do before the stores close."

"We can do all of that to—" I started to say, but she cut my ass off quick.

"Nah, we doing this shit tonight! I've waited long enough and I have all my ducks in a row before G gets back to the city, so waiting until tomorrow is not an option. I'll text you the address so you can come right now."

"Okay, send the address. I'm heading out the door right now, sis."

"A'ight, bet," she said, hanging up.

I grabbed my coat off the coat rack by the door, along with my keys and purse. When I opened the door, I almost shitted on myself. Tonio was standing there about to put the key in the door. Trying to catch my breath, he pusheed me back into the house and closed the door.

"Where are you rushing off to?" he asked, dropping his keys on the glass table. He looked at me with pure lust in his eyes, while licking his lips. I tried not to think about all the dirty shit that was going through my mind. I had to get to Nova because she was adamant about taking care of whatever it was that she had to take care of.

"I'm about to go see Nova. I have to make sure that she is all right with my own eyes. She wants to go home, Tonio. Do you have a key to G's house?" I asked just to see what he would say.

"Nah, ma, I don't. Plus, he don't want her to be alone right now. That's why she is at Rissa's house. But I don't mind you going over there to be with her. Just make sure you go straight over there. Call me when you get there and I will come over there to trail you back home when you are ready to leave," he said, walking over to me.

He pulled me into his arms and kissed my lips softly. I stood on my toes and deepened the kiss, my panties soaking instantly. Pulling away, I had to cut that shit short or I was never gonna get out of that house. I forgot that he was coming over, so I was happy that he wasn't upset. Then again, he knew how much I missed my friend and he understood.

"Okay, baby. Make yourself at home and I will be back as soon as I can. I don't need to you to come get me because when I come back, I want you to be ready to fill my mouth with something long and hard."

He stood there looking at me with the most shocking look on his face. It instantly turned into an evil smirk. He grabbed a handful of my ass and hugged me again.

"Hurry up and bring my ass back then and don't have me waiting all damn night. Yo' ass got a nigga ready to bend yo' ass over that couch over there," he said, nodding his head towards the couch. I took that as my cue to leave. I laughed at him and grabbed the keys off the table and went out the door.

When I got in my car, I started laughing. Dropping his keys in my purse, I started the car. He wouldn't be able to come trail me if he wanted to. He don't have any keys. And I knew he had a key to G's house. They were too tight for him not to have one, but we will find out soon enough.I had a feeling that Nova was trying to pull a fast one, but I would have to wait until I got to her to find out what it was.

As I was driving, I decided to call Jade. She didn't answer, but before I could call back, my phone rang displaying her name. I pressed the answer button and connected the call.

"What's up, boo? You busy?" I asked.

"Busy doing what? Scony is in Atlanta, remember? Nova is still missing and you have been spending all of your time with Tonio. There's nothing left for me to do except work. I'm doing that from home since don't nobody want us to go out into the real world."

"Well, I guess today is your lucky day. I'm about to come scoop you up. I have something to tell you. Be ready in fifteen and I mean fifteen because we have somewhere to be," I said, hanging up on her ass.

167

As soon as I hung up the phone, I received a text. As I pulled up to a red light, I opened it up. It was the text with the address from Nova. I saved it in the Maps app on my phone. The person in the car behind me laid on their horn and I looked up. The light had turned green. I pulled off and continued on to Jade's house.

Hopping on the expressway, I was doing seventy in a fifty-five. I really hoped the Po Pos wasn't out because that was a for sure ticket for my ass. I drove for about ten minutes and got off, turning down the street that Jade lived on and parked outside her house. I saw her look out the window and then she came out. When she got in the car, she looked at me like she was trying to read my mood. I pulled off.

"Where are we going, Mo?" she asked.

I looked at her briefly and turned my head back around, giving the road my undivided attention. "Sit back and enjoy the ride. I have a surprise for you." And that's all I gave her as I started the GPS to get me to Flossmoor.

"Monica Williams! You better tell me what the fuck is going on. Yo' ass is too giddy over there to be doing the shit alone. I wanna be happy, too," she said in a baby voice.

"Sit yo' crybaby ass back and enjoy the ride, Jade. We will be at the destination in about twenty minutes. Believe me when I tell you, it will be worth the wait," I said, turning on the radio to drown her ass out just in case she decided to continue whining.

We sang our hearts out until the GPS said that our destination was on the right. I pulled into the driveway of a beautiful home that looked like it could belong to a celebrity. I checked the address that Nova had sent to make sure that I entered it correctly and I did. I turned off the car and unbuckled my seatbelt.

"Who the hell lives here, Mo? Let me find out Tonio living large like this!" she screamed.

"Get out of the car, Jade, and come on," I said, opening the door to get out. I started walking to the door when it opened and a very young looking woman stood there smiling. That is where G got his looks from. He looked a lot like his mom, but she could pass for his sister. She is the true definition of 'black don't crack'.

When we made it to the front door, she stepped aside to let us in.

"Hello, Mrs. Davenport. I'm Monica," I said, holding out my hand.

"Hey, Monica. Nice to meet you," she said, pulling me in for a hug. It took me by surprise because she didn't even know me to give such a warm welcome. "And you must be Jade," she said, staring at Jade as she came through the door.

"Yes, ma'am. That would be me. Nice to meet you."

She pulled Jade in for a hug, as well, and closed the door and locked it. She led us deeper into her home and it was beautiful. She had a black and cream coordination going on that was put together very nicely. I loved the way that she had all African American artwork throughout her home. We sat on the black sectional that she had in her living room while she sat in the armchair to our right.

"Would you ladies like something to drink?" she asked. We both replied no at the same time.

I wanted to know how much she knew about us. Before I could ask, she was reading my mind.

"I have heard so much about you ladies from those knuckleheads that I call my sons. Monica, from the sounds of it, you are all in my nephew's heart and he is gonna do any and everything to get you to stop fighting what he has in store for you. My advice to you would be to just let nature take it's course and accept the love that has been presented to you. Jade, Jade, Jade! Demarius is a hard one to talk about, but I have to admit, I have never seen him smitten about a woman before. Revoke his hoe card, girl. Whatever you are doing, keep at it. That man used to change women like he changed his draws before he met you. Don't give in to his ass too fast. Make him work for it. I think that's what you have been doing and he's not used to that. I think all of you are good for my boys and I want to see you guys around for the long haul. They need strong women in their lives to keep them grounded and I'm glad that the three of you were chosen," she said, smiling.

"Thank you so much for your kind words, Mrs. Davenport—" Jade started to say, but she was cut off.

"Call me Rissa, girl! Do I look like I'm old enough to be called Miss anything?" she said, laughing.

"No, ma'am, I mean Rissa. But as you know, our friend, Nova, has been missing for almost a week—" Jade was interrupted once more by the voice that she hadn't heard in days.

"Who's missing? I'm right here, sissy," Nova said, walking down the stairs.

Both Jade and I jumped up and ran full throttle towards her. We didn't plan on letting her go anytime soon. We all fell back on the stairs still locked together. We missed her so much and thought she wasn't gonna make it back to us. Tears were flowing like a river from all of us.

"Okay, get y'all behinds up! Y'all forgot that I was just sitting here having a conversation with y'all, huh? "Rissa said, laughing. We all got up, wiping our faces and headed back to the sectional.

"Mo, you know that you are so wrong for not telling me about this," Jade said, wiping her face.

170

"Nah, then it wouldn't have been a surprise, boo," I said, laughing. I turned to look at Nova and her face was a mess. The smile was wiped from my face and replaced with a deep frown.

"Don't even speak on it, sis. It's all good. This is temporary, but you best believe what they got coming will be permenant."

I saw Rissa hold her hand up for me to pause whatever I was about to say. "Nova baby, I know that you are upset and seeking revenge, but once you go down that road, there will be no turning back. Listen to what I'm telling you, baby. You have to think before you react."

"I've had nothing but time to think about the decision that I have made. I'm killing that bitch and that's that. Can't no one change my mind. It's one thing for them to do what they did to me, but that bitch killed my parents! She stood by my side every step of the way through that shit and she was the wolf in sheep clothing. I would never forgive her for that. I asked G for his permission and he didn't not give it, now I'm just gonna do it. No one knows how I'm feeling right now and I'm gonna get justice for my parents in these streets. G is gonna be mad and he may even stop fuckin' with me, but at least that bitch will not be walking around another year thinking she got one over on me. I didn't do shit but help that bum ass bitch and this is the thanks that I get! Nope, not anymore. She is a dead woman walking."

No one said a word after Nova finished talking. There wasn't anything that could be said. Rissa threw her hands up and hunched her shoulders, changing the subject. "What are you girls about to get into?" she asked.

"I want to run to the mall and buy a couple of things, then I have to go to this pawn shop to pick up something."

"Nova, don't be trying to go to the pawn shop to buy a gun, baby. You don't know how many bodies could be on them. If you are gonna buy a gun, buy it new. I'm just saying," Rissa said, rolling her eyes.

"Mama Rissa, I own two guns already and my man have too many to count. I promise you that I'm not going to buy a gun. But we are about to get out of here because it's getting late and I don't want to be out too long," she said, standing up.

We walked across the room toward the door when the doorbell rang. Everyone stopped and looked at Rissa. "Are you expecting anyone, Mama Rissa?" Nova whispered.

"Hell nawl, I'm not!" she said, walking to a monitor that was hanging on the wall. We all walked behind her to look, as well. There was a delivery guy on the porch with a box of some sort.

"Y'all stay right here," she said, pulling her gun from her waistband. I almost started laughing. Rissa was on that gangsta shit.

"Who is it?" she said without opening the door.

"I have a delivery for a Nova LaCour," the guy said in response.

"Who is it from?" she shot back.

The sound of papers rustling could be heard outside the door. "It is from a Grant Davenport, ma'am. Are you going to open the door?" he asked.

Rissa unlocked the door and opened it. The delivery guy was face to face with the barrel of her gun. The expression on his face was priceless.

"Let me see that damn paper and it better be a legit invoice or I'm gonna blow your head off." Her eyes were trained soley on him. When he handed her the paper, you could see the quake of his hand. He was scared shitless.

172

"Come over here, Monica, and look this shit over," she said with her arm outstretched.

I walked over and read the invoice and it was good. "He's a delivery guy, Rissa. Put the gun down and let him do his job. I'm sorry, sir. You can never be to careful now a days," I said.

Rissa lowered the gun, but didn't put it away and the delivery guy started bringing in the boxes. He had a total of five big boxes and a small one. Once he dropped the last box, he handed the invoice to Rissa to sign. Then he ran his ass out of the house like it was on fire. We all started laughing our asses off. That shit was funny and the laugh was much needed.

Nova walked over to the first box and opened it. There was a dozen of the prettiest olive green roses I had ever seen in that box. When she opened the other boxes, the same thing was in each of them, but different colors. There were lime green, aqua blue, purple and baby blue roses. They were so pretty. There was a card attached to one of the boxes and she opened it, but she didn't read it out loud. But the smile that was displayed on her face told it all.

Rissa handed her the small box and she quickly opened it. Inside, there was a Pandora bracelet that was blinged out. You could see the sparkle everytime the light hit it. There was a baby carriage charm that was covered in diamonds, as well as another charm that had a notet engraved on it.

"That is beautiful. My son knows how to spoil a woman. I'm just mad that I have to share that shit now."

Nova laughed, while placing the bracelet back in its box. She handed it to Rissa and turned and grabbed a light ass windbreaker off the coat rack.

"We are out of here, Mama Rissa. If your son calls, please tell him I am sleeping. I don't need him to know that I left out of this house. I know it may be hard for you to lie to him, but I need you to do this for me," Nova said.

"I won't tell him baby, but hurry back and I won't tell him that his words didn't get through to you either. I already know that you are going to go through with whatever plan that you have set. All I can say is be careful, Nova. And we will be going to my doctor in the morning to check on my grandbaby. There isn't going to be any arguing about that."

"Okay, woman. I hear you. We can go to the doctor tomorrow. Now, can I get out of here so I can get back please?" Nova said, giving Rissa a hug and headed to the door. Jade and I said our goodbyes and we left.

Chapter 20

Nova

Mama Rissa was a thug. I could see that she was about that life back in the day and she understood my mindset. That's why she didn't try too hard to persuade me not to go forward with what I had planned. She herself knew that I needed to do this on my own, but she was going to play the role of a mother to say that she tried.

I was sitting in the front seat of Monica's car, heading to the pawn shop. I needed to get a new toy for my mission. The pawn shop wasn't too far from G's house, so it wasn't far away at all. He and his mom lived literally about fifteen minutes away from each other. As we pulled up to the pawn shop, Monica had to ask a question.

"Nova, what are we coming here for?" She was looking at me as if she was going to be able to stop me from making this purchase.

"Come in and see," was all I said and got out of the car. I walked in and there was no one there but me and the guy behind the counter. I had called earlier and got confirmation that they had what I needed.

"Hello, you must be Gary," I said to the man behind the counter.

"Yeah, I'm Gary. How may I help you?" he asked.

"I called earlier in reference to your collection of machetes. I'm here to take a look at them and possibly make a purchase if I like what I see."

"Okay, let me go to the back and bring what we have up front for you."

At that point, Monica and Jade walked through the door. I knew that they were going to try to talk me out of making this purchase, but it will not happen. I had already visualized how I was going to end Ziva's life and it would become reality. Gary came from the back with about eight machetes in sheaths. The first one he took out looked old and in bad shape.

"Shid, you might as well throw that piece of shit in the garbage. Won't nobody in their right mind buy that. Let me see something else."

Every damn one he took out pissed me off. This muthafucka wasted my damn time with this bullshit he had in there. I turned to leave and he was quick to get me to stay.

"Hold on, I got one more for you to see," he said, heading to the back of the shop. Before he could disapear, I stopped him in his tracks.

"I'm going to give you fair warning not to bring back no bullshit. I'm already mad because you have wasted my muthafuckin' time. If you have some good shit back there, bring that bitch to me. I don't have time for your song and dance right now. This shit is not good for business. Now go and get whatever the fuck you are going to get and hurry the fuck up," I said lowly, but stern.

He rushed to the back and I could feel Monica staring a hole in the side of my face.

"Nova, what the hell do you need with a machete? And why did you talk to that man like that?"

"It doesn't matter what I need it for and right now is not the time to discuss it. But did you see that bullshit he brought up here? Would you purchase that shit? Nah, you wouldn't, so can I do what I came here to do, please?" I turned back around just as Gary was coming back. He had one item in his hand and he laid it on the counter. He removed the blade from the sheath and I almost had an orgasm on sight.

"This is a Tang Kukri machete. It is 19.7 inches and the blade itself is 13.33 inches. It is made of durable 3Cr13 stainless steel with black coating. It comes with a sheath with leg straps. There is also a sharpening stone that is included. I can give it to you for seventy-five if you like it."

He explained this machete to me and I was sold. I had looked at this exact machete online, but I didn't want to have to wait for it. But luck was on my side because that bad boy was well over three hundred dollars.

"I'll take it, but for fifty. You weren't trying to give me none of the good shit and had me in here wasting my time. So fifty is as far as I'm going," I said to him.

"Damn, you are hurting me, Miss Lady, but I won't even argue with you. I'll let it go for the price you want."

I looked at him and smiled. I took my debit card from the compartment on my phone case and gave it to him. After he finished the transcation, I gathered my new toy and walked out the door. When we got to Monica's car, I asked her to pop the trunk. I threw the machete in, shut it, then walked to get in. The car was silent for the first couple of minutes, then Monica spoke up.

"Now would you tell me what you need that for?"

I looked over at her and smiled. "I'm gonna cut Ziva's fuckin' head off with it when I catch up with her. Take me to G's house. I need to get some clothes and shit." I turned my head back straight and the smile never left.

***

When we pulled up to G's house, I hopped out of the car fast. I picked up one of the stones that was along the walkway prepared to bust out a window.

"Nova, don't throw that! I may have a key to inside," Monica yelled at me. I turned around and looked at her as she walked up to me at top speed.

"What the hell happened to you, Nova? You have changed. It's like you don't care about anything anymore. You are doing things without even thinking about it first. It's like you are a loose cannon, sis. Please talk to me," Monica damn near begged.

"I haven't changed and didn't nothing happen to me. Kelvin and Ziva just unleashed the bitch in me. Once they are taken care of, then you will get the old me back. Until then, what you see is what you get. I know you heard me back at Mama Rissa's house. That bitch killed my mama and my daddy! She won't get away with that shit, Mo. So everybody needs to stop trying to tell me in very few words not to do it. *I am not taking no for an answer!* So don't start with that shit!" I was beyond frustrated with having to keep repeating myself. "Now, where is the key so I can go in and get my fucking coat?"

Monica fumbled with a set of keys she had took out of her purse. Every key she tried didn't work, so I snatched the keys from her hand and looked at them. I recognized a key and stuck it in the lock. It turned with ease. I opened the door and keyed in the alarm code when I entered. Jade was the last to come in, so she locked the door.

I walked toward the stairs and was met by the sound of Lady whimpering at the basement door. I went to the door and opened it. Lady ran out and tackled me. She was licking me all over my face and running around me with her tail wagging rapidly. I got up and went to the patio door and let her out. She stood by the door, looking at me with sad eyes. I had to tell her to go in order for her to go take care of her business.

While Lady was outside, I ran upstairs to pack a bag and hopped in the shower. I took one of those county showers that took about five minutes so I could hurry up and get out. I went back into the bedroom and grabbed a pink jogging suit and my white AirMax. I lotioned my body down and threw on underwear and socks, along with my jogging suit. Once I put my shoes on, I grabbed my bag and headed down the stairs.

Lady was ringing the bell on the door to be let in. I let her in and went to the basement to make sure she had food and water. After that, I went in the garage to check to make sure nothing was out of place and low and behold, my car was there. I looked inside and everything that I left in there was still inside. I let the garage door up, got in and started up my car. I pulled it out into the driveway and went back inside. I needed my own transportation. I hated waiting for someone to take me anywhere.

"Let's go. Y'all can trail me back to Rissa's house. I'm driving me own car," I said, walking to the front door. They left out and I set the alarm and closed and locked the door.

Meesha

Chapter 21

Kelvin

I had been blowing Ziva's phone up for the past thirty minutes and she hasn't been answering. I was almost to the house in Itasca, but something was telling me not to go. I drove slowly up the road, but I didn't see anything unusual that was out of place. There were no cars on the street either. When I pulled up to my house, the door was wide open. It wasn't dark, but it was dark enough to miss something.

I saw Ziva's car parked in the driveway and I knew that I couldn't leave without making sure she was okay. I pulled in behind her car and jumped out. I was on my way inside the house when I stepped on something. I looked down and it was her phone. I picked it up and I saw all of my missed calls on the screen. Her purse was a couple feet away by the stairs. At that moment, I knew that something happened to her.

I ran into the house and searched high and low. There was no one in there. Nova, Conte, nor Ziva was in that house. That muthafucka was going to see me. He turned on the wrong muthafucka. Conte did the worst thing that anybody could have ever done. He let that bitch go and did something with Ziva. On top of that, his ass took my damn money. I turned off all the lights in the basement and headed out of the house. I jumped in my car and headed back to the city. It was time for me to show my face on the Nine.

I pulled my phone out of my coat pocket and dialed that nigga Conte's number. That muthafucka didn't answer, so now I knew why he was dodging my calls. I sent his ass a text message to let him know that I was looking for his ass.

Conte: *Yo' muthafuckin' ass took my money and freed that bitch! The last thing yo' ass should have done was turn on me! I will be seeing yo' ass, nigga, and when I see yo' punk ass, I'm killin' u, nigga. So u already know when I see u, yo' ass better be strapped.*

I was fuming all the way to the Southside. These muthafuckas was looking for me, well they about to see me. I don't know how the fuck they thought I was a scared nigga. My mama didn't raised no pussies. When I got off the expressway at Seventy-ninth, I pulled in the gas station to get some blunts and gas. When I exited the car, I saw Scony's cousin, Lovely, with her dude, Jerome. The first thing I wanted to do was shoot her ass, but I changed my mind.

I walked over to her and she was looking like a real life Walking Dead zombie. The bitch was so out of it, that she didn't give a fuck what was going on around her. I ran back to my car and popped the trunk. I had about five baggies of crack in that bitch and I'm glad I did. I walked back over to her and spoke.

"What's up, Lovely?"

She looked up at me like she was trying to figure out who I was. I stood there until she open her mouth to say something.

"Who is you?" she asked, scratching the side of her face.

"You don't remember me? I'm Lamont. I used to hang out with Scony back in the day. I'm sorry about your son. I heard about that shit when I got back in town. Where that nigga Scony at anyway?" I was trying to see where her head was at as far as that nigga was concerned.

"I don't know where he at. I haven't seen him in a couple weeks," she said, continuing to scratch different parts of her body.

"Damn, he ain't been checking up on you and shit? I guess what I heard was true then, huh?"

"What the fuck you talking about, nigga?" Jerome asked, licking his crusty lips.

"Word on the street is Scony set that shit up the day your son got killed. He had a hit out on them niggas. They saying that he sent some guys over there to air that bitch out and he didn't give a fuck that your son was over there." I was laying that shit on thick. These two muthafuckas are about to turn on that nigga. At least that's what I was aiming for.

"Scony wouldn't do that to Malikhi. He loved him like a brother," Lovely said with tears in her eyes.

"Well, I'm here to let you know that he did that shit, but here, take this and go handle your lil' problem. I don't want y'all to be out here sick and shit," I said, handing them the five baggies. Both their faces lit up like they won the lottery.

"I thought you should know that your own family killed ya boy. If you don't believe me, ask that nigga. He is gonna deny it, of course, but he did that shit," I said, looking at Jerome.

He had this faraway look in his eyes like he was thinking about being on some dumb shit. I said my goodbyes, went inside to pay for my gas and grabbed my blunts. When I came back out, them two fiends were nowhere in sight. They were on their way to beam 'em up, Scotty.

I finished pumping my gas and got into my ride. When I was about to shift the gears, I received a text message. I looked down at the screen and it was that nigga Conte. I hurried to open the message and read it.

Conte: *Nigga, yo' threats don't mean shit to me. You know where I play at. Come see me. Yo' pussy ass only know how to get with women, nigga. I'm a grown ass man. I haven't been moving funny and I'm not gonna start now. I'm not hiding out from no muthafuckin' body, so when u're ready, pull up, nigga.*

Oh, I see all of these niggas think I'm a bitch ass nigga. I got something for all of they asses. They better be ready when I come through because it's about to be a war. That's what they have been itching for anyway, so why not give them what they want? I was about to pull away from the pump when there was a knock on my window. I turned to see who it was and it was a nigga from around the way named Cisco. I let my window down a little bit, so I could hear what the nigga was talking about.

"Aye, nigga, what's up? I ain't seen you around in a minute. What's good wit ya?" he said, looking around.

I knew that it was cold as hell, but this nigga was looking kind of nervous and shit, like he was on some bullshit. I reached in the driver's door and grabbed my .380, I wasn't about to let this nigga do shit without at least putting something hot in his ass.

"I've been chilling. What's been going on out here? Shit been kind of hot, so I just stay in the cut, you feel me?" I was trying to figure out what his body language was trying to tell me, but I couldn't read this muthafucka.

"When I saw you over here, I wanted to come and let you know that there is a bounty on yo' head, nigga. I fucks with you the long way and I wouldn't be a real nigga if I didn't let you know what the word is in the streets."

"Who the fuck got a hit on me?" I wanted this nigga to confirm what I already knew.

"The Goon Squad, man! I don't know what the fuck you did to them niggas, but they were out asking anybody they saw if they had seen you. Oh yeah, they even had yo' sister, nigga. I don't know if they did anything to her, but I know I saw her get in the car with one of them niggas. I can honestly say that I haven't seen her since. And Mrs. Diane had to go get the kids from school because BB didn't pick them up."

184

This nigga had my head all fucked up with the shit that he just told me. My sister didn't have a damn thing to do with the bullshit that was going on, but they insisted on fucking with my family to get to me. I picked up my phone and dialed BB up. The phone rang, but she didn't pick up. I tried a second time and got the same results.

"Aye, good looking out. I'm about to get out of here. If you see BB before I do, tell her to hit my line. I appreciate you telling me everything, man," I said, putting my car in gear.

"Man, if you need me to help you with them niggas, let me know. I want to knock these niggas off anyway because they making too much money out here. I got an army of niggas that would be willing to come along for the fight. All you have to do is let me know and I will set that shit in motion."

"Do that shit, my nigga. Let me get a number on you. I am definitely gonna need your team on this one. Them niggas killed my mama and my brothers, man. Now you telling me that they got my sister, so yeah, this shit is real personal." He hit me with his number and I locked it in my phone. "Be looking out for my call, my nigga. I hope you ready to go to war because it's about to get messy in the hood," I said, driving off.

I tried hitting my sister up again and this time she answered.

"Hello."

"Aye, sis. What's this I hear that them muthafuckas from the Goon Squad had you in their car?" I waited for her to respond because if she said some stupid shit, I was going over there to beat her ass.

"Are you serious right now? You calling me like I'm fuckin' one of them niggas. I was in that fucking car because of your stupid ass! What the fuck have you done? Them niggas was about to blow my muthafuckin' head off behind

185

some stupid shit you did! But all you worried about is what *you heard?* Get the hell off my line with that shit. I don't fuck with you because of the situation you put my mama in, nigga! So I don't give a fuck what happens to yo' dumb ass. Just stay the fuck away from me and my kids," she screamed and ended the call.

My sister was pissed the fuck off and she had every right to be. Them muthafuckas held a gun to her head probably trying to find out where I was, but obviously they didn't know that BB didn't fuck with me no more. I would be damned if I allowed them to keep harrassing her, though. I'll kill a muthafucka before I let them kill another member of my fuckin' family. I already knew that them muthafuckas had Ziva. She don't go anywhere without her phone. The scene at the house in Itasca just didn't look right. Deep down, I was praying that she got away and will be calling me soon.

As I was driving, I decided to get the fuck out of the city. I got on the expressway heading to the 'burbs. I was thinking about all the things that had happened today, from that nigga Conte snaking me, Nova getting away, Ziva calling me stupid then not answering her phone, finding out that the Goon Squad got a hit on a nigga and last but not least, these niggas going after my family. I didn't know what I was going to do, then a thought came to mind and I started laughing out loud. I had planted the seed at the gas station. I had an inside connect and her name was Lovely.

Chapter 22

MaKenzie

It felt good to finally have that throw down with Demarius. I've been wanting to punch his ass since the doctors came out of that hospital room and told us that my granny didn't make it. He had been MIA for months and it pissed me off. Oh, excuse my manners. Let me introduce myself. My name is MaKenzie Jones. I am the youngest of Demarius' twin sisters. My sister, MaKayla, and I are like two balls to a dick. We are inseparable. I am the twin that has a no bullshit attitude, standing at five feet five inches tall, one hundred forty-five pounds and cute as hell. Being twenty years old and making my own money makes a bitch feel real good. There's not many young women that can say they are getting money without a nigga giving them that shit.

My brother thinks his money is the reason I live the way I do. Nah, he got shit twisted. I told him that niggas were taking care of me, but that's far from the truth. My brother and G taught me and my sister how to hold, clean and shoot a gun at an early age. I don't know what possessed them to teach two little girls how to do that shit, but I'm glad they did.

They also made sure that we knew how to defend ourselves with our hands and stressed to us often about not taking no shit from none of these niggas and bitches on the streets. We both took heed to the things that we were taught, but if they knew what me and my sister really did for money, they would fall dead. Good thing he would never find out because that's not for him or anyone else to know.

I was in my room packing up so we could get this house sold. I had to find me a place to live quickly because I couldn't continue to live in this house. My granny put all the love into this place and I wouldn't be a home without her here. As I threw clothes from the closet to the bed, there was a knock on my door. I paused before I invited whoever was on the other side in. "Come in," I yelled.

MaKayla walked in and closed the door behind her. She looked around and made room on the bed, taking a seat.

"Kenzie, what the hell was that all about downstairs? Are you out of your mind? That's our brother that you pulled a gun on! You already know that you don't pull a gun unless you plan to use it!" she screamed.

I didn't know where she was going with her rant, but I wasn't trying to hear that shit. "I told his ass to leave me the fuck alone! Then he put his hands on me, so I did what he taught me to do. He punched my ass and I reacted accordingly! The reason he isn't being placed in a body bag right now is because he is my brother and I love him that much! I wouldn't have given two fucks if it was a nigga out there!" I screamed, pointing toward the window. "I should've shot his ass just to show him that *I am that bitch*!"

I couldn't believe she came in here trying to question my get down. Of all people, she knew how I rolled. Shit, we are one of the same. I had to calm my nerves before I went off on her ass. I was wrong for threatening to shoot my own flesh and blood, but the nigga hit me!

"Kenzie, calm down. All I'm saying is don't do that shit again. I don't want it to come to this, but if I have to, I will beat yo' ass. It's us against the world, that includes Demarius," she said, rolling her eyes.

"Well, I advise you to go have the same conversation with his ass because if he comes for me again, I won't make any promises that I won't shoot his ass the next time around," I shot back.

MaKayla sat there, shaking her head. She already knew that I could go all day with this shit. I tolerated many things and disrespect wasn't one of them. "Well, since we got that out of the way, I need to talk to you about something."

I nodded my head for her to continue.

"Demarius came to me and said that he wanted us to go back to Chicago to live with him." I didn't let her finish what she was trying to say. I jumped in immediately.

"I'm staying right here in Atlanta! My granny isn't here to make me leave! That's the only person that would be able to tell me to go back permanantly and that won't be happening. I'm sorry, Kay, this is my home. If you want to go back to Chicago, that's fine, but I'm not. I'm going to bury granny and I'm getting the hell out of there." I went back to cleaning out my closet.

There was another knock on the door and I let out a long sigh. I guess this is the meeting spot for the ones that were in their feelings.

"Come in," I yelled once again. Demarius walked in with G on his heels. I rolled my eyes and kept taking clothes out of the closet.

"I kind of heard y'all in here talking and I thought this would be a good time to let both of you read this."

Demarius held out a piece of paper and Kay took it. She started reading it and looked over at me. I walked over to where she was and we started reading together. The tears started rolling down my cheeks, blurring my vision. I wiped my eyes and continued reading. I could hear my granny's voice in my head with every word I read. When I finished reading the letter, all I could do was hug my sister.

"We are gonna be okay, sissy. She explained everything in this letter for us, now we can move on the way she would want us to. You read what she said. She don't want us to cry

189

or be sad. She's all right where she is. It's gonna be hard, but we will make it," MaKayla whispered in my ear.

I heard what she said, but I was still angry. In my mind, my granny was supposed to live forever. She was never supposed to leave me, but I knew that I had to let her go in order for her to be totally free. I just didn't know when I would be able to do that. She stated she wanted us to go back to Chicago, so I guess I had to do what she wanted. I looked up at my brother and the tears continued to cascade down my face.

"I'm sorry for pulling that gun on you, but don't you ever put yo' hands on me again. I damn sure won't hit you either. I knew that once I hit you, the consequences weren't gonna be good, but I asked you to leave me alone," I said to my brother.

"Kenzie, you had been avoiding me since I got here. We needed to talk. I wasn't about to let you walk out of here without doing so. What happened between us was bound to happen because you bottled your feelings inside. You can always come to me to talk. I will always be here for you."

He walked over and wrapped me in his arms. Kissing me on the top of my head, he let me go. "We will be leaving sometime tomorrow. Everything has been taken care of for Grandma Liz. We are in this together. Y'all don't have anything to worry about, okay?" Both my sister and I nodded our heads yes.

"G, I have something that I want to talk to you about when you get a minute," MaKayla said, looking across the room at him.

"Speak on it, sis. We don't need to talk in private."

MaKayla looked at Scony, hunching her shoulders. "I know that we talked about this already, but would you at least consider letting Nova handle that bitch that did her dirty? I won't stop talking about it until you give the okay. But if you don't, that bitch is gonna die regardless by the hands of yo' girl whether you say yay or nay. Now I tried to respect yo' word, but y'all always taught us that you take the garbage out when it stinks. Let her have this, G. Let me talk to her."

"Wait a fuckin' minute. What the hell is going on? What are you talking about, Kay?" I looked around the room and both G and Demarius was shaking their heads. "Somebody say something. Don't leave me in the dark any longer," I said, folding my arms over my chest.

MaKayla started telling me what she was referring to and I was getting mad listening to the words that fell from her lips. When she finished I didn't hestitate to put my two cents in on the situation.

"So, you mean to tell me that you aren't gonna let her handle this shit after what they put her through, G? I understand that she is pregnant and you're worried about the baby, but do you actually think something is gonna happen to her with us there? Nah, it's not gonna happen. We need to talk to her to see where her head is at. If I sense that she isn't capable of dealing with the job that she wants to carry out, I'll talk her into letting me and Kay handle that hoe, but if she is down with the murder game, she is gonna handle that shit on her own. I won't let you take that from her. She's entitled to that shit. They violated in the worst way."

"How the fuck are y'all gon' sit up here and tell me what the fuck I'm gon' do? Like I told her ass, it ain't happening. When we get to Chicago, the Goon Squad is gonna handle that bitch. That's all I have to say about it," he said, walking to the door.

"We will see about that shit. She's at Rissa's house, right?" I asked with a smirk on my face.

G turned back around with his face was scrunched up. "Don't call my mama's house on that bullshit, Kenzie. I'm not playing with you."

"Kenzie, let us handle this, please. Y'all don't need to be getting in no kind of trouble when we get to Chicago," Demarius said.

I just looked at him and laughed. I walked to the dresser and grabbed my phone. I dialed Aunt Rissa number, waiting for someone to pick up.

Chapter 23

G

I stood at the door, watching MaKenzie on her phone. I was pissed she went against what I had said to her. I didn't want Nova to kill anyone. Once you start killing, you keep killing. That's not the life I want for her. She was innocent when it came to this street shit. The less she knew, the better. It was a different story when it came to Kenzie and Kay. We trained them the same way we trained the Goons, but I didn't want that for My Future.

"Hey, Aunt Rissa. How are you?" Kenzie said, putting the phone on speaker.

"I'm fine, baby. How are you guys holding up down there?"

"We're doing all right. We will be heading that way tomorrow. Everything has been handled on this end. We will have to come back down to clean the house out completely, but other than that, we are pretty much set to go," she said into the phone.

"That's good to hear, baby."

"Auntie, I called to speak to Nova. Would you put her on the phone, please?"

"Yeah, hold on a second." The sound of her putting the phone down could be heard. My mama was the only person I knew that still had a house phone. A couple of minutes passed before the phone was picked back up and Nova was on the line.

"Hello," she said softly in the phone. MaKenzie looked at me with a look of defeat in her eyes. I told her that Nova wan't about that life. Now I was glad she did call. She wouldn't push her to do something that she knew she wasn't capable of.

"Hey, Nova. This is MaKenzie, Scony's sister." She stood quietly waiting for Nova to respond.

"Okay, I'm sorry about your grandmother. My condolences to you guys," she said quietly.

"Thank you. I know you don't know me, but I heard about what happened to you and I wanted to reach out and talk to you. My sister kind of heard the conversation that you were having with G earlier and I need to know if you were serious about what you said."

"Am I serious? You're kidding me, right? Did Grant have you to call me to try to change my mind? If so, tell him that he can kiss my ass! There will be no talking me out of shit!" Gone was the soft spoken woman that I fell in love with and in her place was Satan himself. I looked at Scony and he had a look of surprise on his face.

"No, no, no! G didn't have me to call you at all. As matter of fact, he was against it. I called because I wanted to hear from you what happened to you. Would you mind telling me, please." Kenzie looked at me with that smirk on her face again. I wanted to see if Nova's tone was gonna go back to the one that I knew oh so well. It didn't.

"To make a long story short, my supposed to be best friend hit me over the head with a bat and put me in a muthafuckin' trunk. My stupid ass ex went along with the shit, took me to this house out in the middle of nowhere and had me tied to a damn bed for four fuckin' days. He beat me in my damn face and threatened to take my pussy. Ziva's stupid ass confessed to fuckin' my daddy and my ex for years, but she never expected me to get out of that house alive. She killed my muthafuckin' parents and I'm killing that bitch for it. G can either be by my side when I end that hoe's life or he can call the police and move on with his. Nothing will stop me from getting justice for my parents." Nova could be heard breathing hard into the phone.

Kenzie took that time to continue to talk to her.

"I agree with you that justice should be served to both of them. I will be in Chicago tomorrow and shit will get handled as soon as we touch down. We will be out looking for her ass, so she better hope she got out of dodge. With that being said, I'll see you tomorrow, chica. And it was nice talking to you. We can get to know each other better after we handle this business," Kenzie said, ending the call.

Kenzie looked at me and threw her phone on the bed. "Do that sound like a woman that's unsure about what she wants? We killing that bitch with or without your permission, case closed. I will be there to watch that bitch take her last breath."

Before I could respond, my phone rang. I thought in my head that it was Nova calling, but it was Tonio.

"Yo, cuz. What's up?" I put the phone on speaker and leaned against the wall.

"It's about damn time you answered yo' muthafuckin' phone. I've been calling you and that nigga Scony for the longest time with no luck getting either one of y'all."

"I didn't get a call from you, fam," I said, looking at Scony.

"Shit, I didn't get a call from you either, Tonio. I don't know what the fuck was going on."

"Well, I got y'all now, so let me fill y'all in on what's been going on down here. The lil' goon I had watching the house that Kelvin had Nova at, got ahold of that bitch Ziva." My eyes instantly went to the twins and they were happier than a muthafucka hearing that shit. Tonio continued talking. "I got her ass tied to a chair at the Dungeon, awaiting y'all return. I'm not even gonna go check on that bitch, cuz. Fuck her. I

195

almost popped her ass to be honest, but I know sis wants to handle that shit on her own. I think you should gon' head and let her get that shit off."

"That's what's up, cuz. I don't think I have a choice but to let her take care of her business. There's too many of y'all against me on this shit. We will rap about when I touch down. Any word on that nigga Kels?"

"Nah, ain't nobody seen nor heard from that nigga and his sister hasn't called either. But I don't think she is on any grimey shit, though. She is still living her life like she's been doing, taking care of her kids. That nigga ain't been by her crib either, so I think she was telling the truth about not fucking with his ass. Oh yeah, Scony. I saw Lovely, man. Cuz out there bad, my nigga. I saw her and that nigga Jerome over there by her old crib smoking that shit. She is looking like she has been smoking that shit all day everyday, my nigga. You are gonna have to track her ass down when you get back. We have to save her from herself."

"Man, I already know. She checked herself out of rehab a couple of weeks ago. She is gonna be next on my list after we handle that other shit at the Dungeon. But good looking out, fam. Let her do what she's doing for now. I got her when I get back fo' sho'," Scony said, running his hand down his face.

"Is there anything else that we should know about?" I asked Tonio.

"Nah, that's all I got for now. I'm gonna get off of here. I'm going over to see Monica in a minute. Jade is missing the hell out of you, Scony. That damn girl is looking like she lost her damn dog or something. Call her, man. I know you haven't because I know how you are. No need to respond tho. I'm out," he said, ending the call.

I looked at the twins and shook my head. "It's on when we get to the Chi. Don't make me regret my decision," I said, walking out the door.

I called Nova, but she didn't answer. I wasn't about to call my mom's line, so I went in the guest room and took a shower and laid down.

I didn't remember falling asleep, but at some point I did. I reached and grabbed my phone and saw that I had eight missed calls, all from Avah. I thought about if I should call her back or not. Deciding to call, I pressed on her name to dial her number. Shit, it was four in the morning and I was calling a woman that wasn't My Future. I had to tell her what I was doing before she found out on her own. I didn't know how she would take it, but I had to put it out there. I didn't have no feelings for this broad. I was just trying to get close to that nigga, Kelvin. After that, the bitch was a done deal.

"Why are you calling me so late, G?" she said, whispering into the phone.

"I just woke up and I saw that you had called me several times, eight to be exact. I wanted to make sure that you were all right. What's up?"

"I was trying to see if you were back in Chicago yet. You haven't called to say anything and I can't get in touch with my girl. She hasn't been answering her phone."

"Nah, I'm not back yet, but I'll be touching down tomorrow. I have a few things to handle when I get back, but I will definitely hit you up when I'm ready to see yo' ass. Believe it or not, I miss you, Avah." I had to lay shit on thick as hell to get her to trust me. She still didn't know that I knew about her involvement with Kelvin.

"G, you have a woman. You don't miss me," she said, smacking her lips.

"I'm not with her anymore, Avah. Why the fuck do you think I'm trying to make shit right with you? I fucked up choosing her over you, I realize that now. Are you gonna let me right my wrong or are you gonna keep fighting me with this? I'm not about chasing no females, so you better get it while the getting is good, ma."

"I hear you, G. I'll see you when you get back. I still love you, baby," she said lowly.

"And I love you too, Avah."

I threw that back at her and hung up. Yeah, I need to tell Nova about this shit. I rolled over and went back to sleep.

***

I woke up when I heard someone banging on the bedroom door. I rolled over to grab my phone. It felt as if I had been asleep thirty minutes. When I looked at the time, it was well after noon. I fell back onto the bed and my phone rang in my hand. I looked down at it and it was Scony calling.

"What nigga?" I said with my eyes closed.

"You need to get up and wash ya dirty ass balls and brush ya damn teeth. Everything is set to take granny home, nigga."

I sat up and swung my legs out of the bed. Walking to the door, I unlocked it and pulled it open. Scony was standing there with the phone still up to his ear, waiting for me to say something.

"What time are they gonna be ready to roll out?" I asked.

"They said we should be at the airport at three."

I stood there and looked at this nigga like he had eight heads. His stupid ass was standing in front of me still talking to me on the phone. I shook my head and kept looking at him.

"Did you hear what I said, nigga? You ain't answering me, dog."

"Answer one question for me, bro. Why the fuck are you still talking into that muthafuckin' phone and I'm standing right here in your face? You about the dumbest nigga I have ever seen in my life," I said, laughing so hard that I had to grab my stomach. I couldn't stop laughing to save my life, I got a cramp in my side and still couldn't stop laughing.

"Nigga, I didn't even realize I was doing that bullshit. Fuck you, man! That shit wasn't funny. You should have said something sooner."

That only made me laugh harder because why should I have to tell this nigga that he was talking to me on the phone and in my face at the same damn time? I turned around and ran to the bathroom. I laughed so hard I almost pissed on myself. I drained my lil' dude and washed my hands. When I went back to the door, that nigga was gone. I closed the door and chuckled back to the bathroom.

I took care of my hygiene and threw on a pair of jeans, a long sleeve black thermal shirt and my black Tims. I put on my diamond Jesus piece, my diamond stud in my ear and my diamond bracelet on my wrist. I sprayed Gucci Black on my clothes and I was ready to start my day. I gathered everything that I had in the room and packed it in my luggage. I grabbed my luggage and headed downstairs to see where everyone else was. Putting the luggage by the door, I went into the kitchen. The smell of bacon and eggs had a nigga's stomach growling like a muthafucka.

"It's about damn time your high yella ass woke up, sleeping like you're the one pregnant and shit."

"I see yo' ole waterhead tail got jokes, huh? Where is my breakfast, woman?" I asked, while sitting down.

"Negro, your ass slept through breakfast and do I look like your damn woman?" she said with her hand on her hip. I wasn't trying to hear that shit. I knew damn well she had a plate in the microwave for me. "Yeah, just what I thought. You better get your ass up and fix a bowl of Cap' n Crunch," she said, walking out the kitchen.

I jumped up and open the microwave, empty. I checked the oven, empty. I even looked in the refridgerator, nothing. I was lowkey pissed. I grabbed a bowl and fix me some damn cereal. I was eating slow as hell because that's not what the hell I wanted. I looked up and Scony's ass was standing in the doorway to the kitchen laughing.

"What the fuck yo' ass laughing for?" I said, dropping the spoon in the bowl.

"How's that cereal, brah? Is it hitting the spot, my nigga?" he said, busting up with tears running down his face.

"Fuck you, nigga! Do it look like I'm enjoying this shit? Get the fuck on, Scony," I said, getting up to dump that bullshit in the toilet. I didn't even want to eat that shit. When I walked out of the bathroom, this nigga looked at me and started laughing again.

"What the fuck is so funny, man?" I said, grilling his. I was pissed off because I was hungry as fuck.

"The same shit that was funny earlier, nigga. That damn bacon was good as fuck the second time around. Not to mention the eggs, grits and those b-b-b-butter biscuits. Nigga, don't you ever play me as a fool again. Payback is a muthafucka," he said, laughing his as off.

I didn't find that shit funny at all. I put the bowl in the sink and charged his ass. I picked him up and slammed him on the floor, grabbing him in a headlock. We were rolling around on the floor when we heard Aunt Sarah's loud ass voice.

"What the fuck is wrong with you two fools? Get y'all ass up right now!" she screamed.

We kept right on wrestling, ignoring her ass. This nigga ate my damn breakfast. I wasn't about to let his ass go. I felt a stinging sensation on the back of my leg, so I let his ass go and rolled on my back. This crazy ass woman had a thick ass fireman belt in her hand and she had hit my ass with it.

"Aunt Sarah, what the fuck is wrong with you?" I screamed.

"Didn't I tell y'all hardhead muthafuckas to stop?" she said, slinging the belt at Scony and caught him across his back.

That nigga stretched like a damn cat. I started laughing because it took me back to when we were kids. I saw her draw back to swing the belt again and I jumped up. Scony was still feeling the effects of the last hit, so he was slow. She caught his ass again and he jumped up.

"Sarah, I will beat yo' old ass. Hit me with that damn belt again! I'm a grown ass man. What the fuck I look like letting you whoop my ass with a belt?"

"Oh! And you cussing! I'm about to beat yo' ass for real now," she said, running up on him.

I took that opportunity to charge her ass and pick her up. I threw her ass on the couch and tried to wrestle the belt out of her hand. She was not letting it go for nothing, so I stopped trying and started tickling her ass.

"G, if you make me piss on my mama couch, I'm going to beat yo' ass like you stole something. Stop, dammit!" she screamed between laughs.

When I was about to stop, I felt someone jump on my back and Scony started screaming at the same time. Makenzie was the monkey on my back and Makayla had kicked Scony in the same leg Aunt Sarah popped his ass with the belt. He tackled Kay and I flipped Kenzie. This went on for damn near an hour. We were tired as fuck when we realized that it was time to get to the airport. We all needed that little bit of fun. Now it was time to get to the Chi and pay our final respects and wreck some shit.

Meesha

Chapter 24

MaKayla

The ride to the airport was very quiet. The realization was setting in, at least for me it was. My granny was really gone. I tried my best to keep the tears at bay and so far they were cooperating. I looked out the window when we pulled into the airport and saw the hearse that held my granny. I turned my head because I didn't want to continue to look at it. The funeral home wanted to take her on a commercial flight, but Scony wasn't having that, he wanted her to ride with him.

I didn't get out of the car until they put the casket on the plane. Once they had everything settled, Scony came to the car to get me. I laid my head on his side as we walked to the plane. When I stepped inside, my body relaxed. I felt my granny's presence instantly, but I refused to look toward the back of that plane. I took the first seat I saw in the front and Scony was right by my side.

"Are you all right, Kay?" he asked, hugging me.

"Yeah, I'm all right, brah. I wanna go with you when you go out to look for Lovely. I already know that you are gonna beat the streets of Chicago to find her," I said, looking at him. He was staring straight ahead with a look of disapointment on his face.

"I am gonna go out to look for her without a doubt. That's my cousin, man, and she has a promise that she made to her son that she has to uphold. I'm gonna make sure that she keeps that promise. I'm not worried about that right now. We have to take care of that business at the Dungeon and get granny settled in her final resting place. I'm gonna try my best to find Lovely before the memorial. She needs to be there."

203

"Demarius, you can't save someone that don't want to be saved. Lovely has a mind of her own and you're gonna have to let her live her life the way she sees fit. You can't make her stop using drugs. She has to want to stop. I suggest you get some insurance on her ass. She is going fight you tooth and nail about that heroin. I would hate to have to kick her ass if she want to be on some dumb shit. That's my cousin, but the drugs are speaking for her right now and I don't know that hoe."

"Let me handle this, MaKayla, please. This is not an outsider. Lovely is family, so we don't need to be in beast mode for this one."

"I hear what you're saying, but don't let the bitch get out of line because family or not, I will drag her ass. When a muthafucka on that heroin they transform into a Power Ranger and I will knock her out like a Transformer. I'm not gonna play with her ass at all. I don't trust a junkie any day of the week." And he knew that I wasn't joking about what I said. I don't play about my brother.

We sat and talked about some of everything. When he started talking about Jade, I looked at my brother and my heart swelled. I never thought I would see the day that my brother fell for a woman, but it seems like this woman had won him over. I couldn't wait to meet her. I'm gonna have to take her out for a celebratory drink. Her ass winning and I bet she don't even know it. Before we knew it, the lights of the Windy City could be seen below.

"Fasten your seatblets, ladies and gentlemen. We will be landing in Sweet Home Chicago shortly," the pilot announced over the system.

I turned to Scony and grabbed his hand. "Are you ready to paint this bitch red? It's time to show you what I'm made of.

MaKenzie, Nicassy, and myself is just what the Goon Squad needs," I said, laughing, but I was very serious.

"Get the fuck out of here. Y'all ain't ready to be Goons. Y'all got so much more to learn, baby sis. I'll make sure to train y'all myself to get y'all ready for these mean streets of Chicago," he said, chuckling while patting my hand.

If he only knew about the Atlanta Twins, Storm and Tornado, with their side kick Hurricane I thought, laughing to myself.

Meesha

Chapter 25

Scony

The wheels of the plane touched down on the pavement with a heavy thud. We were finally back in Chicago and I was glad. I couldn't wait to see Jade. It was six o'clock in the evening and I hadn't talked to her since I left. I hoped she didn't fuck my house up. I know I was wrong for not reaching out to her, but I wanted to have a chance to miss her. I was gonna make sweet love to her ass and she was gonna get stuck after this dick lashing. Yeah, I had plans for that ass, but duty calls first.

When the doors to the plane opened, MaKayla was trying to jump over me to get off first. "Slow down, baby sis. They are gonna wait until we get off before they take her off. Calm down, baby. It's okay." I had to hold her because she was breathing too fast. She started crying and I couldn't do anything but hold her.

After she calmed down, I stood and let her haul ass off the plane. I grabbed our bags and got off the plane, as well. Tonio was standing by his truck, rocking Kay back and forth. It was starting to hit her now and I knew I had to be strong for them. When everyone got off the plane, the funeral director stepped off and they started bringing the coffin out. I hurried to put the twins in the truck. I heard them start screaming, so I stuck my head inside the truck to see what was going on. Nicassy was getting smothered by both of my sisters. The three of them together was trouble in the making.

I closed the door to let them have their moment. Turning to watch my granny's coffin being placed in yet another hearse, I watched it drive away until I didn't see the headlights anymore.

"You good, brah?" G asked, walking over to me giving me a brotherly hug.

"Yeah, I'm good. Let's go get sis so we can end this bitch life. It's time to silence her ass and let that nigga know that the Goon Squad is back and his ass is next in line," I said, hopping in the truck.

It's a good thing Tonio's truck was big enough to hold all of us or we would have been tight as hell in that muthafucka. Nicassy and the twins were talking a mile a minute, Aunt Sarah looked like she was ready to fall on her face, and G and Tonio were up front just chilling. This was my family right here. A few were missing, but we were all we had and I loved it.

We dropped Aunt Sarah off first, but all of us men got out and made sure we did a walk through of her crib before we left. I gave her a hug and told her to contact me the minute she heard from Lovely. When we got back in the truck, the talk of what was about to happen began.

"So, what's the plan for this bitch?" Tonio asked, lighting a blunt and hitting that bitch hard.

"Head to my Mom Dukes' crib, cuz. I have to go scoop up My Future," G said, staring straight ahead. Tonio glanced in his direction briefly before giving the road his attention.

"You really gonna let cuz take care of Ziva's ass? I don't think it's a bad idea. They put her through hell these last couple of months."

"Yeah, I'm gonna let her handle the bitch, but I don't like it at all. I'm gonna give her the opportunity since she's been so pissed off about it. I lost the hand on this one, so I threw them up. I just hope she can live after this shit. Y'all all ready know how it is for some with their first kill, but I will be there for her after this shit," he said, taking the blunt from Tonio.

208

"I hate to be the one to tell you that I think you're wrong. Nova is more than ready to off this bitch, cuz. That's all she was talking about. I don't think she will have an ounce of remorse. She even told Monica that she was eliminating that bitch. I didn't give Monica one clue that I already found Ziva, so this is something that she don't need to know."

"I agree. Don't tell her and Jade shit. Let they ass stay innocent. Nova was forced to be a beast. This is what them muthafuckas wanted when they put her through all that bullshit. Now Ziva is about to see the monster they created, up close and personal. I don't think she is about to play with her ass tonight," I said.

"Well, I can't wait to see what she got in store for this dirty bitch. The shit that she told me that happened had me wanting to kill her myself. But I'm gonna sit back and wait for my turn. I think I'm gonna get that nigga for y'all. It's taking y'all too long. I got just what he need, some pussy," MaKenzie said.

G and Tonio started busting out laughing. I didn't' see a damn thing funny. "Shut yo' ass, Kenzie! Don't let me hear yo' ass say no shit like that no mo"! I screamed.

"I'm just saying, y'all pussy footing around with this nigga. I'm just letting y'all know that I got what y'all need to trap his ass."

"And I'm just saying, shut the fuck up." Her ass knew that she had pissed me off, so she started back talking to Nicassy.

"Scony, fix yo' fuckin' face, man," G laughed as we pulled up to Rissa's house.

"Fuck you, nigga! Did you call Rissa before we just popped up over here? Yo' ass know damn well yo' mama is trigga happy," I said to the back of his head.

"Y'all worried about my mama. I'm not," he said, getting out of the truck, he walked to the back door and opened it.

"Well you walk yo' ass in front. Everybody else stay behind that nigga. If she starts bustin', hold his body as a shield." Everybody started laughing as we walked up the steps. G reached in his pocket and took out his keys, but the door opened before he had the chance to put it in the door.

"There's my baby!" Rissa said, hugging his spoiled ass like he's been gone for years. I glanced down at her hands and there was nothing in them.

"Ummmm, Rissa. Can we come in out of the cold, please? You can baby his ass some more when we get in that warm house," I said, fucking with her like I always do.

"You can stay yo' dreadhead ass right there on the porch and freeze, muthafucka," she said, pointing her finger at me.

I laughed at her while she hugged everybody. When I stepped up to the door, I was laughing. I reached out to hug her and she slapped the fuck out of me.

"Cuss at me again, asshole. I'm gonna slap the shit out of you again," she said, hugging me and rubbing my jaw at the same time. When she let me go, I slapped her on her ass.

"What the fuck I told you about touching on my muthafuckin' mama, nigga." G got mad every time I did that shit.

I only did it to piss him off.

"Man, shut the hell up. Rissa, can you explain something to me?"

"What, nigga?" she said with her hand on her hip.

"Why is it that everytime we come over here without G, you pull yo' gun on us, but when this nigga come and stick his key in the door, he gets hugs and shit?" I stood there with my hand holding my chin, waiting on her reply.

"Cuz you aint my baby, nigga! Case closed," she said, walking away.

I couldn't do nothing but laugh. Her ass was funny as hell. I loved me some Rissa, but I knew how far to push her. She was crazy as fuck.

"Hey, Ma. Where is Nova?" G asked, coming out the kitchen.

"She's upstairs sleeping. She said she was tired. That's one hardheaded ass woman. I told her ass that we was going to the doctor to check on the baby and she agreed, but we ain't been yet. You better talk to her ass before she sees my true colors around this muthafucka," she said, sitting on the chaise that sat in the corner of her living room.

"I got it, Ma. I'm back now. She will definitely go to the hospital. I'm gonna take her myself," he said, running up the stairs.

"I hope that nigga don't get lost up there, with his soft ass." I barely dodged the pillow that Rissa threw at me. She hated for anyone to say anything about that nigga.

Meesha

Chapter 26

Nova

I went upstairs to sleep after Mama Rissa fed me good. We had baked chicken, mashed potatoes, string beans, Hawiian rolls and homemade sweet tea. After my last bite, I felt my eyes getting heavy. If I stayed here another day, I was going to be as big as a house before I delivered this baby. I was dreaming about G licking my kitty. I haven't had sex in a good minute and I was horny as hell. This dream seemed so damn real. I was trying to wake myself up, but it wasn't working. It was dark and I could really feel the orgasm in my stomach. A moan escaped my mouth, my back arched and I gapped my legs open wider. My hand went under the cover to massage my clit, but when I felt a head down there, I tried to push it away.

I threw the covers back, but I couldn't see who it was because the room was dark. I wasn't dreaming after all. This shit was actually happening. The only person that has been to Mama Rissa's house was Tonio. Lord, please, don't let this be my man's cousin snacking on my cookies like this. Another moan escaped my lips and I tried to scoot away from the unknown mouth, but my thighs were grabbed holding me in place.

"Oh shit! I'm about to cum! Please let me go!" I pleaded.

"Well, cum for me, baby."

That voice made my heart cry. That was the voice of my baby. My nectar flowed like the Mississippi River and he did not let up. He kept right on feasting, licking me from my asshole to my pussy. I had to grab the pillow and throw it over my head. I was about to explode and I knew I was going to scream in ecstasy. I didn't need his mama hearing me go crazy over the head her son was dishing out. I thrusted my hips upward, feeding him my love. He didn't miss a beat. He had a death grip on my pearl.

"Arrrghhhh! Yes, baby. Eat that shit, baby. Here it come. It's cumming, baby. Yes, right there. Right there, baby. Babbbbbyyyyy!" I screamed into the pillow and I kept cumming, even after he stopped.

Kissing me from my kitty to my stomach, I continued to cum with every kiss he planted on my body. When he reached my lips, he kissed me long and hard. Our tongues intertwined and I tasted delicious on his lips. I reached for his pants and he tried to stop me, but I wasn't taking no for an answer. I needed him to fuck me.

"Baby, please! I need you," I said into his mouth.

"We have somewhere to be, baby. There are people downstairs waiting on us. I got you when we get home," he said, kissing me again.

"No, we can get a quickie in. We have time for that," I said, breaking free of his hold and grabbing his dick. He moaned into my neck. I knew I had him then. I made my move and unbuckled his belt and his jeans. He sat up and pulled his pants down, spreading my legs and pushing them back. He got comfortable between my legs and dove in.

"Oh shit, this pussy tight as fuck and its gushy as hell. Ahhhhh, shit, Nova!" he said, pumping hard with each stroke.

He pulled out and tapped his dick on my clit. He was trying not to cum too fast. But I already knew when he went back in it was gonna be over for his ass. He turned me on my side, holding my left leg up and went in balls deep. I had to bury my head in the pillow once again. I threw my ass back at him, meeting him thrust for thrust. He was using my breast as leverage and tweeking my nipples at the same time.

"Oh shit! Fuck me harder, G! Hit that shit and stop babysitting my cat! Hit it," I said through clenched teeth.

He went crazy after I said that and he was beating it up just right. My love tunnel tightened up around his pole and with me throwing this pussy on his ass, his back went rigid and we came at the same time. He flopped on his side and curled up behind me, kissing the back of my neck.

"I missed you so much, baby. I love you."

"I missed you too and I love you more," I said, getting up to go to the bathroom. I jumped in the shower and washed up quickly and took a soapy towel in the room to wipe him off. When I touched his lil' dude, he shot right up, looking me in my face. My mouth got watery as hell. He open his eyes and shook his head.

"Nope, go rinse the towel and bring it back. We have to go, baby. We have been up here long enough." Just as the words left his mouth, there was loud banging on the door.

"Get y'all nasty asses out of there right damn now! That's why your ass got a baby in your stomach. Ain't no fuckin' going on in my house unless it's me that's doing the fuckin'! Y'all got five minutes to get down them stairs."

Mama Rissa just clowned on us in front of whoever was down there. I wanted to laugh so bad, but we had about three minutes to get downstairs now. We then rushed to get ourselves together. I had put on a black Nike jogging suit and my black Hurraches and I pulled my hair in a ponytail. I was making sure my hair was in place when Grant started talking to me.

"Baby, I have something to tell you. I don't want you to get mad either because there's nothing to it," he said, rubbing his head.

"What are you trying to say, G? The way you are beating around the bush trying to soften the blow, you got me thinking you've been up to no good" I stared at him with my eyebrow raised.

He cleared his throat. "I reached out to Avah and agreed to meet up with her. I was thinking I could use her as a way to get to Kelvin, but baby, I'm gonna have to play this shit right. I have to make her think that I love her."

I stood there for a spell and the words that fell from my lips surprised me.

"Let me tell you something. I love you, Grant, and there is nothing on this earth that can stop that. I trust you with everything in me and I don't have a problem with you using the bitch as bait, but you will do it by following my rules. You can take the bitch out on the town and wine and dine her ass and I'll even pay for the shit. You can even fuck her ass and make her sing like a bird, but you will strap the fuck up! There will be no kissing under any circumstances and don't fall in love with the bitch. That's all I have to say about that situation. Oh, break the rules and I will kill yo' ass myself," I threatened, walking out the room. He didn't have a chance to say anything in return, so he just followed me out. When we got downstairs, all eyes were on us.

"Damn, brah. What took y'all so long?" Scony asked with a smile on his face.

"Nova wasn't feeling—" G started to say before his mama cut him off.

"If your ass lie in my house, I'll slap the shit out of you. How the hell she don't feel good when you got a hickie on your neck that wasn't there when you came in this muthafucka. Let me find out that sucking on your ass makes her feel better."

My face turned ten shades of red when she said that shit. Everybody busted out laughing, even Mama Rissa.

"Don't be embarassed now. It was your ass that gave away what the hell y'all was doing. Hit that shit, baby. Yes," she said, mimicking what I was saying during our session.

I was standing there, wishing the floor would swollow me whole at that moment.

"Okay, it's time for us to go," I walked over to Mama Rissa and tried to give her a kiss on the jaw.

"No the hell you won't! I don't know where your lips been up there screaming like that. Y'all have fun," she said, patting me on the back. "I know damn well y'all ain't leaving all these damn flowers in my house. This ain't the Botanical Garden. Take that shit with you."

"I will take them when I come back. Nova has to get her things anyway," said G.

"Don't come get them and watch me throw them in the garbage. Play with it if you want to, Grant."

"Okay, Ma. I heard you, I'll see you in a couple hours," he said, walking to the door. Everyone said their goodbyes and headed out of the house.

***

We got outside and walked to the truck that was in the driveway. One of the females that was with them turned to me and introduced herself.

"Hey, Nova. I'm MaKenzie. It's good to put a face with the voice. Are you ready to do this?"

"Hello, MaKenzie. What are you talking about?" I turned to look at G.

"We're about to take you to see Ziva. Are you ready?" asked another female.

I didn't know who she was, but she had to be MaKenzie's twin because they were identical.

"Uh, who are you?" I questioned.

217

"I'm sorry. I'm MaKayla, Mackenzie's twin if you haven't noticed. And this is Nicassy." She pointed to a third woman. "She is our sister from another mother. Now answer the question. Are you ready to let us see your get down?"

Once again, I looked at G to see if this was a joke. He had been adamant about not letting me kill her, and now I was being told that I could finally gut that bitch like a fish.

"Yes, baby. That's where we are going. You can thank the twins and Tonio for this shit. I still don't want you to do it, but if you think you can, go for it. But I want you to know if you freeze up in any way, I'm taking you out of there," he said, looking me dead in my eyes.

"Deal! Give me a minute, I have to grab something out of my car," I said, stepping over, and to the back of my vehicle.

When I reached it, I popped open the trunk and pulled out my new toy and grabbed my Nina, putting it in my waistband after checking the clip.

From a few feet away I saw my man's forehead crease. "What the fuck do you have, Nova? And how the fuck did you get your car here?"

"I have my ways, but don't worry, you will see what I have when we get to our destination. Let's go. I've been waiting for this shit." I damn near ran to the truck and hopped in, as my heart thumped with nervous anticipation.

The others piled in behind me, one by one. As soon as the doors shut and we drove off, Scony spoke. "Damn, sis. You happy as a kid on Christmas and your face cleared up nicely. I'm glad I didn't see what it looked like before."

"Thank you. I'll let you see it when the time is right, but I am happy this lil' girl had a lot to get off her chest when I was strapped to that bed. I want this hoe free as a bird when we get there. I don't want her to be helpless. That's some coward shit. I want her to fight back."

218

It was as if a whole different person had invaded my body. For now, the good girl was gone. In her place was a treacherous bitch hell-bent on revenge.

"Nova, I didn't agree to that shit. I agreed to you killing her ass, not fighting. You are carrying my baby, if something happens—" I stopped him right there.

"That scary non-fighting ass bitch ain't gonna get a chance to react. Believe me on that shit. Nothing's gonna happen to me or our baby, I promise."

"Okay, baby girl, I'ma let you do you." He shook his head in disbelief at my determination to handle that hoe without his interference. Sighing, he said, "I gotta hit Quan up and tell him to meet us at the Dungeon. Conte too."

I sat quietly, staring out of the window as he made those calls. My hands were folded in my lap, but my mind was a collage of painful memories that Ziva had caused in my life.

I felt a tear slide down my face.

"Baby, you sure you're okay?" asked G, gently.

"I'm about to be." *Once I hand deliver a heavy dose of Karma to that ratchet hoe.*

G nodded his understanding, almost as if he could read my thoughts. I knew he was battling with himself because he didn't want any blood on my hands. But the gangsta in him had to understand how much it would mean to me to slump that bitch.

We drove the rest of the way in silence. Twenty minutes later we reached the warehouse where shit was about to get go down. I was super excited. Tonio stopped the truck and cut off the engine. He got out and went to unlock the door. Everybody piled out of the truck and stood there for a minute before we all filed inside one after another.

G and I were the last two to walk through the door. He turned and locked the door and moved further into the warehouse. There were five quick bangs that could be heard on the door. Tonio went to open it and Quan and Conte walked in. I had to thank both of them for what they did for me, but it wouldn't be right now.

"Welcome to the Dungeon, ladies and Conte. Only Goons have blessed this place and lived to tell about it. But I'm here to let y'all now that no one, and I mean *no one* is to know about this place. Y'all are only here because of Nova. Is that understood?" G asked, looking at each of us.

I shook my head yes and Conte agreed, but the three troublemakers didn't respond.

"I'm in this muthafucka because I'm a muthafuckin' Goon!" MaKayla said with her hand on her hip. The men chuckled, but the women didn't find it funny at all.

"The joke will be on all y'all in due time. Trust me when I say y'all need us." Malaya stated.

This time all three of the girls laughed at the men this time.

I wasn't trying to do all of that hee hee ha ha shit. I was ready to get to what I came there for. I walked over to Ziva and she looked up at me and smiled, like she held no fear.

"Hey, bestie. How are you? I see your face is healing nicely. Do it still hurt?" she mocked, licking her lips.

There was a puddle of piss under the chair. I wondered how long she'd been there, but that shit was irrelevant right now. What was muthafuckin relevant was the smirk on her face. I was going to wipe it off and smear it all over the floor!

"You already know that yo' snake ass ain't no friend of mine, but that's neither here nor there. What you are gonna do is tell me where the fuck Kelvin is." I blasted.

"I'm not telling you shit!"

"Wrong answer, bitch." I punched her in the mouth, damn near snapping her neck. "Now, let's try this shit again. Where the fuck is Kelvin?"

"Fuck you, stupid bitch. Y'all ain't never gonna find him. He is gonna start poppin' you muthafuckas off one by one. So get ready to die, all of you wanna be tough muthafuckas." Blood ran from her busted mouth.

"Oh, you tough?"

I hit that bitch with a round of punches that made her ass start leaking on impact. I wasn't playing with that hoe. I held eye contact and promised her she was gonna die slow.

She held her head down and didn't raise it again. I walked up to her and pulled a knife out of my pocket. Breathing evenly, I bent down to cut the rope.

"Nova!" G yelled my name and I cut my eyes at him.

"I told you in the car that I got this shit. Let me do me, baby," I shot back.

"I hear you, but you don't have to do this. I'm your man!" He pounded his chest with his fist. "All you have to do is fall back and stay beautiful, have my seed and chill, I'll handle punk ass hoes like her. You're my future; you're not a killa. Fuck letting you do this shit."

He walked up and held his hand out for me to give him the knife. I didn't want to defy him or test his authority as my man, but I would never have peace in my heart if I didn't slay Ziva myself.

I looked up into G's eyes, pleading. "Baby, please don't break your word to me. You know everything she's done. She killed those that were close to my heart. Please, G! Please!" I choked up with raw emotion.

G's eyes watered at my pain. He turned his head away for a brief second to recompose himself. When he looked at me this time, it was with forced resignation. "Okay, this what you

221

want?" He huffed, and then continued on without allowing me to answer. "When this shit haunts you in your sleep, don't say I didn't warn you, because it will. Unless you're heartless, taking another's life will stay in your mind every hour of the day and night. You'll see."

"Maybe I will, but I'll deal with it."

I turned from him and faced the bitch who had turned me cold. "Now, it's time to reap what you sowed."

I cut the rope from the her right leg and she tried to kick me. I caught that bitch and dug a hole in her calf.

"Aaaaaaaarghhhhhh! You stupid bitch! What the fuck is wrong with you?" she screamed with tears running down her face.

"Didn't I tell you that I wasn't the same bitch you grew up with? You should've taken heed to that shit. Now I'm gonna cut the other muthafuckin' rope off your other leg and, bitch, if you attempt to kick me, I'm gonna break that muthafucka. So I hope we have an understanding around this bitch."

I went to cut the rope and the bitch spat in my face. "Fuck you, you dirty bitch!"

I stuck my finger in the wound and twisted that muthafucka around.

"Arrrrrrrrghhhhh! Bitch, you crazy!" she yelled in between cries.

"You didn't know? This is the bitch you created! You wanna keep testing my gangsta? Keep going down the road you started traveling. I have more where that came from," I said, laughing at her ass. I cut the rope and stood up. I swung the blade and sliced her across her face.

"Owwwwwww! Shit!" She screamed loud as hell.

"That's for spitting on me, you nasty ass bitch. Back to the question at hand. Where the fuck is Kelvin Deshaun Banks, Ziva?" I asked through clenched teeth.

222

She started breathing fast, her chest rising and falling at rapid speed. I stood there and waited. She didn't say anything, so I started counting down from ten.

"10, 9, 8, 7, 6, 5, 4, 3, 2—"

Before I could get to one, she decided she wanted to talk.

"Okay, hold on. He has an apartment in Riverdale on 144th & Normal. The address is..."

I listened while she gave up the info.

"Now I told you what you wanted to know, would you let me go?" she pleaded.

"Did you get that, baby?" I said, looking over at G.

"Baby, we already knew that address. He hasn't been there in a minute, so that shit ain't nothing new," he said nonchalantly.

I turned back to Ziva and I walked to the right side of the chair and cut the rope in the back. The rope fell and now she was free to go. I walked back in front of her and put the knife in my pocket. She attempted to stand and fell back on the chair. I looked around and spotted a bandana on a table in the corner. I walked and picked it up.

"Tie this around your leg," I said, throwing it in her lap.

She did what I told her to do and stood up. She went to walk past me and she swung and missed. That gesture right there opened the door for me to fuck her up. I punched her in the eye and gave her two quick punches to the side of the head. She was dazed for a second, but she came charging at me like a bull. I stepped to the side, grabbed her jacket in the process and rammed her head into the wall and let her go.

She got up and limped toward me with her fist up. I laughed out loud and I didn't recognize the sound, but I knew it came from me. She swung and I caught her arm and intertwined it with my own and fucked her ribcage up. I heard a crack and knew I broke at least one.

223

"You should have listened when I told yo' bitch ass that I didn't play with other people's kids." I punched her three times in the mouth. She fell, spitting out blood and a couple of teeth.

"Damn, Nova ain't playing with this bitch. Remind me not to get on her bad side," Scony said, while laughing.

I was tired of talking to that hoe and she didn't know shit else about Kelvin's whereabouts, so she was wasting my time. She wasn't doing shit, but pissing me off.

I walked over to the door and picked up my new baby. I took the machete out, letting the sheath flutter to the floor.

"That's what the fuck I'm talking about! Beast mode! This is the shit I came to see," MaKenzie yelled, jumping up and down.

"Nova! Nova!" G screamed.

I heard him, but I tuned his ass out and continued in the direction Ziva was still sitting on the floor.

"Now, I want to you to tell me the story about you killing my mama and daddy. And I want to hear it the same way you said it when I was bound to that muthafuckin' bed."

"I was lying." She tried to deceive, but I knew better.

"Bitch, don't muthafuckin' insult me!" I raised the blade over me head threateningly.

Immediately, she recounted the story in a shaky voice and it only made me mad hearing that shit the second time around. I swung the machete and cut her muthafuckin' foot off.

"Arrrrrrrggggggghh!!" She screamed so loud, it echoed off the walls.

"What the fuck!" Tonio screamed.

"I didn't tell yo' hoe ass to stop telling the story. I'm listening. I need to hear how you forced my parents into oncoming traffic, bitch!"

She started tellling the story again. I stood there listening. She got to the part about forcing my parents' car into the drunk driver and I walked over to her and drew the machete back. She raised her hand, trying to shield her face, but I didn't give a fuck. I chopped that hoe's arm off. I hadn't come in there to play with her. I was out for blood; in a crazed, murderous zone.

"Aaaaaarrrrrggggghh, Nova! I'm so sorry for eveything," she cried, looking at her arm and foot detached from her body.

"Yes, you are correct. You are one sorry piece of shit. That's the most honest thing you have ever said since I've known your stank ass," I threw back at her.

"G, stop this shit, brah. I have never seen a muthafucka take their time cutting a muthafucka up. She is gonna need counseling, nigga," Tonio screamed, but G didn't utter a vowel.

"One more thing before yo' stupid ass bleed out. What did I tell you I would do to yo' ass if I got out that bed? I'll wait."

After a few seconds, she finally started talking just above a whisper. "You told me that you was—"

"Bitch, I'm gonna need you to speak the fuck up so the niggas in the back can hear yo' slimy ass!" I yelled at her ass.

"You told me that you was gonna cut my head off like the snake that I am and piss down my throat," she said with tears rolling down her face.

Before she could blink, I raised the machete. "*Sayonara*", I sang, meaning goodbye mockingly, before cutting that bitch head clean the fuck off.

Looking down at her decapitated head a few seconds later, it hit me that I was now a malicious murderer.

Maybe so, I said to myself, *but they turned me into this. I did to her what she did to mine. An eye for an eye.*

I had no regrets. If it haunted me in my sleep it still couldn't compare to the grief I suffered over my parents murders at her hands. In my mind, I had avenged them with pride.

"Bitch, you can't haunt me!" I spat, and then I turned around and walked towards the door, picking up the sheath along the way and leaving out of that muthafucka.

Character 27

G

It had been two weeks since we laid Grandma Liz to rest and Nova had killed Ziva. I still couldn't believe how My Future killed that bitch. I took her home that night and catered to her. I ran her a bubble bath, washed her from head to toe and gave her a full body massage. I had to make sure she was mentally okay, but she was fine with the outcome. Watching her boss up the way she did had my dick on swole. That was the best sex I had ever had in my life. We finally went to the doctor to check on my baby. Nova was almost eight weeks pregnant and the baby's fine. She didn't have any prenatal pills, but we were going to be on top of that shit. It was all about my baby.

We had been looking high and low for Kelvin's ass, but he was ghost like a muthafucka. That nigga wasn't anywhere to be found, but he could only hide for so long. We had been lookiong for Lovely just as long. She didn't make it to the memorial or burial for Grandma Liz and that hurt Aunt Sarah badly. We had to sit her down and explain that Lovely would show up when she was ready. I put word on the street that if any muthafucka served her any dope, they were going to die. If she can't get that hit, she will bring her ass back to family. Scony was ready to murk a nigga or two for selling that shit to her. I hope she found her way back before it was too late.

"Baby, hurry up. We got to go!" I yelled.

Nova was in the shower taking forever, knowing that we had to get out of this house. She was in there singing along to every damn song that came through the damn speaker. She better not use all the damn hot water.

227

Today was Thanksgiving and everyone was spending the day at Aunt Sarah's house. The ladies were over there all day yesterday cooking. There would be a house full of folks, so they had to cook a lot of food. It was going to be hard without granny, but we are going to try to make the best of it. She would want us to still have a good time as if she was the one that did all the cooking.

Nova emerged from the bathroom wrapped in a towel. I looked at her thighs and they were getting thicker than a muthafucka. Her hips were spreading and her ass was getting bigger, too. But the one thing that I loved the most were her breast. Now them jokers were getting bigger by the day. Every time I saw her naked, I just wanted to bend her over. I didn't give a damn where we were.

"You like what you see, Mr. Davenport? Close your mouth. You're drooling, baby. Do I need to get you a bib when I go shopping for the baby?" she said, laughing. She climbed up on the step stool to get in the bed so she could oil her body up. She was having a hard time getting in the bed and I couldn't even help her right away because my eyes were trained on all that ass.

"Um, can you please help me and stop molesting me with your eyes?" She stopped trying and turned her head in my direction. Getting her a higher stool was something that I needed to do soon. Her short ass always had trouble getting in our bed. I walked over to where she was and picked her up. I held her for a minute, kissing on her lips. I placed her down on the bed and started rubbing her thighs.

"I'm sorry. It's not my fault yo' ass was all out for me to see. It looked good enough to eat. Can I get a taste?"

"Nah, brah. We got to get up out of here. Isn't that what you were just hollering about five minutes ago? Yeah, that's what I thought," she said, smacking her lips.

"Why are you bringing up old shit, tho? Fuck it, let me get in this bathroom so we can go."

Turning away from her, I stomped toward the bathroom. "Hurry up and put on some damn clothes, too. Got yo' ass out teasing a nigga and shit!" I slammed the door so hard, I thought the windows would crack. I was pissed because she was being stingy with her cookies. She knew I wanted that shit. Pregnancy pussy will have a nigga acting out of character and I am a prime example.

"Awwww, baby. Don't be like that. I love you," she yelled. I didn't even respond to that shit. She wanted a muthafucka to sweat her ass. Nah, she better go out there and get her one of those soft niggas to do that shit. She got the wrong one right here.

I took care of my hygiene and hopped in the shower. My pipe was hard as fuck. I had to handle this shit. I closed my eyes and thought about her evil ass and let one loose. I watched my babies go down the drain. I felt like I had just cheated on her stingy ass. I hurried and washed and hopped out, grabbing my towel. I wrapped it around my waist and went into the bedroom to get dressed.

My baby laid my cream-colored sweater with a pair of blue jeans and my black Gucci loafers out. Once I was dressed, I went downstairs. Lady was following Nova around the kitchen. That was a sure sign that Nova has been feeding her table food again. She had on a cream sweater dress that stopped at those thick ass thighs that I loved so much. She paired it with some black thigh high Dolce boots. Damn, My Future looked good and she was all mine.

I stood lusting over her in the cut. I couldn't stop admiring her. But that lust turned into anger when I saw what she was about to do. Nova had made herself a bacon, lettuce and tomato sandwich. I watched her reach for the plate that had more bacon on it and she was about to hand it to Lady.

"If you give her that got damn bacon, I'm gonna kick yo' ass!" Stepping into the kitchen, she was stuck with her hand out. Lady was creeping towards it like I didn't see her ass.

"Lady, sit!" Even with me raising my voice, she kept going.

"Lady, come here!" I said loudly again.

She looked at me and laid down, looking at me with sad eyes. I looked at Nova and she had ate the piece of bacon and started in on the first sandwich. All I could do was shake my head. She treats Lady like she is a human child and not a dog.

"What have I told you about feeding her the food that I could be eating my damn self? The food that I buy for her lil' spoiled ass is called dog food for a reason. She is a fuckin' dog, Nova! Stop playing with me before you and your dog be living in the basement."

She turned around and looked at me and said, "There is nothing wrong with giving her a little table food every now and again, baby."

"Nova, I said don't do it. There will be something wrong with it if she gets worms, walking around this muthafucka shitting them out. Yo' ass is gonna be the one cleaning that shit up and you are paying the vet bill."

"Why would you say that shit while I'm eating? You make me sick," she whined, pushing the sandwich away from her.

"I don't know why your ass eating anyway. We are about to go to a house that has food for days. Lady, get out of my kitchen, now! Go!" I said, pointing to the basement door. She looked up at Nova and I took a step towards her and she jumped up, hauling ass.

"You didn't have to raise your voice at her, Grant. She's just a baby," she said, rolling her eyes.

230

"Hurry up and finish eating. We have somewhere to be," I said, walking out of the kitchen. Lady was supposed to be a watch dog. Now she is the total opposite. She is Nova's dog.

Meesha

Chapter 28
Scony

I had been beating the streets looking for Lovely since the day after we got back home. I didn't know where the fuck she was, but I gave up. I'm not looking for her ass another day. If she wanted to be out in the street that bad, I was going to let her do what she chose to do. I have one life to live and I'm going to live it. It took me a couple of days to get my mind together to concentrate on Jade, but through it all, she never left my side. That only made me fall for her even more. She met my sisters and they got along really well and that's what I needed, my woman and my sisters to get along.

When I called Jade after I left the Dungeon that night, she was at her house. I had Tonio drop me, MaKayla, MaKenzie and Nicassy off over there. We sat and talked for a couple hours before I took the girls to Nicassy's. I returned to Jade's house and I showed her how much I missed her. We have been sexing like rabbits ever since.

We were trying to get ready to go to Aunt Sarah's for Thanksgiving dinner, but the way my tool was set up, I had Jade bent over the kitchen table.

"Ah, shit, girl. Stop squeezing my dick before you make me cum. I'm not ready to cum yet."

I snatched out of her and dropped to my knees. I started eating her kitty from the back and she moaned loudly. She lifted her leg and planted her foot in the chair. She opened up so I could get all that pussy in my mouth. I wrapped my lips around her clit and sucked softly. Her legs started shaking, so I knew that she was about to explode. I stood up and put my rod back in her sweet tunnel.

"Yes, daddy. Fuck me," she moaned, throwing her ass at me. I hit her with a couple of long slow strokes before I sped up.

"Ssshhhhhit, ooooowwww," she moaned, while biting her bottom lip.

I continued pumping, while gripping both of her ass cheeks. I eased my thumb into her ass and she started bucking hard against me. I felt my nut building and at the same time her pussy was wearing my tool like a glove. A few strokes later, both of us came at the same time. I had sweat dripping down my chest and I was trying to catch my breath. The sex between us was the best that I've had in a long time. I knew this was the woman I wanted to be with. Not because of the sex, but for the love that I had for her.

Smacking her on the ass, I said, "Come on, we have to get showered and dressed to get to Aunt Sarah's. I told G that we will be there when him and Nova showed up. Plus, I want to get there before everyone else so I can set up those tables for Aunt Sarah."

"Okay, give me a minute. As a matter of fact, you use the bathroom in the bedroom and I'll use the one down the hall. You already know if we shower together, we will not make it to dinner," she said, laughing.

"You are absolutely right about that with your sexy ass. Now bring that ass on before I dive back in that good shit. You still in that face down ass up position like that's what you waiting on," I said, laughing.

"Whatever, Demarius. You are just nasty," she said, chuckling while making her way to the stairs.

She lifted her leg to go up and I crawled right behind her, biting her ass. She took the stairs two at a time to get away from me. All I could do was smile because she made this house a home in a matter of months and I couldn't wait to fill it up with a couple of babies.

***

We pulled up to Aunt Sarah's at the same time G and Nova did. It was cold as fuck out here. I think the weatherman said it was going to be like twenty-three degrees today. Shit, it felt more like fifteen. When G got out the car and walked around to open Nova's door, I smiled. My nigga was finally happy and the woman that was by his side was the reason. In the last couple of months, I had seen so many different sides of that nigga behind this woman. All of them weren't good, but I can tell you it showed he did have a heart. He has someone to share his life with now besides his mama and I'm happy for him.

"What's up, brah," he said as he walked up, giving me a brotherly hug.

"I can't call it. Hey, sis. How you and my nephew doing?" I said, giving Nova a hug.

"Now how the hell are you gonna assume that it's a boy, Scony?" she said, cutting her eyes at me.

"I'm not assuming shit. I know you got a boy up in there. We Goons, dammit. What the hell are we gonna do with a girl?" I said, laughing.

"What does that mean? There are plenty of female Goons in the world. They aren't all men, you know."

"You got that shit right. Yo' ass showed my ass that a woman is capable of getting her hands dirty just as much as the next man. I was kind of impressed actually. You're gonna have to teach me how to swing a machete like that one day." I dapped her up and started laughing.

"Leave that shit back at the Dungeon, nigga. Ain't gone be no mo' of that shit. That was a one time deal. My wife will not be your personal trainer, nigga."

235

"Yo' wife? Let me find out y'all went and got married and didn't tell a nigga." I was hoping like hell G didn't say that they did. I was going to whoop his ass!

"Nah, brah. You know I wouldn't do that to you. Shit, you would have to stand in line because my mama would be fucking me up first. It's cold as fuck out here. Let's go inside and we can continue to talk in there." He grabbed Nova's hand and led her up the stairs.

Opening the door to the house, there was music playing and a couple of my cousins had started a spades game. The aroma of food made my stomach start growling. I hung my coat in the closet and reached my hand out for Jade's. She wasn't paying me any attention because she was talking to Nova. So I walked over to her and took it off for her. She looked at me and smiled. I planted a wet sloppy kiss on her lips and hung her coat in the closet next to mine.

I was heading to the kitchen when my cousin stopped me. "Aye, cuz. What's happenin'? Who is that fine ass chick in that red sweater over there?" he said and pointed to someone behind me. I turned and looked in the direction that he pointed and smiled.

"Oh, that's Jade. Why, what's up?" I asked.

"Damn, shorty fine as fuck. Do she got a nigga? If not, I want you to introduce me to her."

"Oh shit, hold on. Let me get her." I walked over to Jade and whispered in her ear. I told her that I wanted to introduce her to my cousins. We got back to the table, I made the introductions.

"Jade, this is Derrick and Derrick, this is my woman, Jade." The thirsty smile that was on his face vanished quickly. He looked at me and shook his head.

"Yo' ass always on that bullshit, Scony. How the fuck you gon' have me thinking yo' ass was about to hook me up?"

236

"I didn't' have you thinking shit. You assumed I was about to hook you up. I told you that I would introduce you to her," I said, laughing.

"Man, get yo' ass away from me. Nice to meet you, Jade. Watch this nigga, he sneaky. Did you know that he was a hoe before you came around?" he said, laughing.

"I've heard about his many woman, but that was before he met me. Now he is a one woman man. How many of those women have he introduced you to?" she asked Derrick.

"Shit, I haven't met none of their asses."

"My point exactly. I'm here to stay, so there will not be anymore women," she said, kissing me and walking away. I followed her ass until she sat down next to Nova. They looked over at us and started laughing. I knew Jade was telling her what had happened.

The front door opened and the twins and Nicassy came in loud as usual. They stopped to speak and hug Nova and Jade. Then all of them started dancing to that damn Cardi B song. I went into the kitchen and Aunt Sarah was in there with Rissa.

"Hey, my two favorite women in the world. How y'all doing?" I said, walking to the both of them kissing their cheeks. "Happy Thanksgiving."

"Happy Thanksgiving to you too, Demarius. Where's my son? Is he here yet?" Rissa asked.

"Yeah, he's in there with everybody else," I told her.

As soon as the words left my mouth, G and Tonio came walking in the kitchen.

"Hello, my beauties. Happy Thanksgiving," he said, hugging both of them at the same time. Tonio following right behind him doing the same.

"Hey, baby. Is everyone here now? Where are those damn twins?" Aunt Sarah asked.

"They are here. They are in there talking to Nova, Jade and Monica, as well as everyone else that's in there. Everyone is here except Lovely," G said.

"Well we are not gonna worry about that. Go tell everyone to wash up so we can eat."

Aunt Sarah started carrying dishes to the table in the dinning room and all of us helped. The table was beautifully set and I couldn't wait to get my eat on. We had collard greens, candied yams, ham, turkey, macaroni and cheese, chitterlings, string beans, dinner rolls, cornbread, dressing, cranberry sauce, sweet potatoe pies and a variety of cakes.

Everyone had washed up and was seated, waiting for the word to dig in, but Aunt Sarah had something that she wanted to say first.

"Thank y'all for coming over to celebrate Thanksgiving with me. I am so thankful to have all of you in my life. Without y'all, I don't know how I would be able to get through these days. Losing my mama, y'all granny, was hard on us all, but she is here with us everyday all day. But I wanted to thank y'all for checking on me and making me smile. I love y'all."

"And we love you back," we all said in unison.

"Rissa, would you do the honors of blessing the food, please?" Aunt Sarah said, looking at Rissa.

Rissa shook her head yes. "Everyone, bow your heads. Let us pray. Lord Jesus, thank you for—"

The sound of the door opening and slamming shut got everyone's attention. All heads were raised and turned toward the entryway, waiting to see who had came in the house. When Lovely walked in, there wasn't a closed mouth at that the table. She had a coat on that was filthy, shoes that looked like they were two sizes too big and her hair was all over her head. Her eyes were sunken into her head and the bones in her face were pertruding badly. I stood up and started walking towards her.

"Lovely, where have you been? I've been looking all over the city for you. I've been worried that something happened to you."

"You ain't worried about me, Scony. You wasn't worried about me when your ass set that shit up to have my baby killed."

I looked at her with a confused look on my face, but before I could say anything she started going off again.

"You didn't think I would find out, did you? I knew when the shit happened that you killed my baby, Scony," she said, starting to cry.

"Now wait one minute, Lovely. You know damn well Demarius didn't have shit to do with what happened to Malikhi," Aunt Sarah said, standing up.

"Wait a minute, Aunt Sarah. I got this. Sit back down," I said, not taking my eyes off of Lovely. "Lovely, where the hell did you get that from? You know damn well that I loved Khi like he was my own son. I took care of him, so why would I kill my own flesh and blood?" What she said hurt my heart. I would never do anything to hurt anyone in my family.

"Don't stand there and act like you and G didn't do that shit! My baby is dead and it's y'all fault!" she screamed.

"Hold the fuck up, Lovely! Don't throw my name into this shit. I did for Malikhi just like Scony did. When yo' ass needed anything, I was there! So I'm not gonna sit here and let you try to run my muthafuckin' name through the mud. Y'all may not be my family by blood, but I consider y'all just that, family! I don't know what the fuck yo' ass been smoking, but you need to lay off that shit. We didn't have shit to do with Malikhi getting killed. Whoever told you that information told yo' ass a lie!"

G was mad as fuck and I couldn't say shit about it. Lovely is throwing accusations around like she knew this shit for a fact.

"Who told you that shit, Lovely?" I asked calmly.

"I know it's true because your boy Lamont told me," she said with her hands in her pockets.

"Lamont? I don't even know a muthafuckin' Lamont," I said, getting mad myself.

"He said that he use to roll with you back in the day. He also said that you were the one that set that shit up and he felt I needed to know. He drives a grey Chrysler 300." After she said that shit, anything else she said went in one ear and out the other. That muthafuckin' Kelvin done struck again.

When I focused back in on what she was saying, all I saw was Lovely lunging at me. I stood there to take whatever hit, slap punch, or kick she was gonna throw at me. But when she got close to me and swung, I felt a sharp pain in my chest. I looked down and there was a red circle forming on the left side of my chest with the knife still sticking out. Then she pushed me back and snatched it out. I stumbled a couple of times, then fell on my knees. Jade was by my side when I fell over, clutching my chest.

"Oh my God! She stabbed him! Call the paramedics! Call the paramedics! Scony, open your eyes, baby!" she cried.

I opened my eyes and saw Lovely running out of the door. MaKenzie and MaKayla ran after her. I knew Lovely was about to die. My sisters didn't play when it came to me. Nova kneeled down beside me and applied pressure on my chest with a towel.

I tried to talk but it was hard, but I knew I had to tell G to get the twins.

"G, G," I whispered.

"G, he keeps saying your name," Jade said.

G bent down low so he could hear me.

"Go find the twins. They gon' kill her, man. Go find them and take care of them for me, man. I love you, brah." Then everything went black.

To Be Continued...
A Distinguished Thug Stole my Heart 3
Coming Soon

Stay Connected with Us!

Text **LOCKDOWN** to 22828 to stay up-to-date with new releases, sneak peaks, contests and more…

Thank you!

BOW DOWN TO MY GANGSTA

By **Ca$h**

TORN BETWEEN TWO

By **Coffee**

BLOOD STAINS OF A SHOTTA

By **Jamaica**

WHEN THE STREETS CLAP BACK

By **Jibril Williams**

STEADY MOBBIN

By **Marcellus Allen**

BLOOD OF A BOSS **IV**

By **Askari**

BRIDE OF A HUSTLA **III**

By **Destiny Skai**

WHEN A GOOD GIRL GOES BAD **II**

By **Adrienne**

LOVE & CHASIN' PAPER **II**

By **Qay Crockett**

THE HEART OF A GANGSTA **III**

By **Jerry Jackson**

LOYAL TO THE GAME **IV**

By **T.J. & Jelissa**

A DOPEBOY'S PRAYER **II**

By **Eddie "Wolf" Lee**

Meesha

TRUE SAVAGE **III**
By **Chris Green**
IF LOVING YOU IS WRONG… **II**
By **Jelissa**
BLOODY COMMAS **III**
SKI MASK CARTEL
By **T.J. Edwards**
BLAST FOR ME **II**
By **Ghost**
A DISTINGUISHED THUG STOLE MY HEART **III**
By **Meesha**
ADDICTIED TO THE DRAMA **II**
By **Jamila Mathis**

Available Now

RESTRAINING ORDER **I & II**
By **CA$H & Coffee**
LOVE KNOWS NO BOUNDARIES **I II & III**
By **Coffee**
RAISED AS A GOON I, II & III
By **Ghost**
LAY IT DOWN **I & II**
LAST OF A DYING BREED
By **Jamaica**
LOYAL TO THE GAME
LOYAL TO THE GAME II

244

LOYAL TO THE GAME III

By **TJ & Jelissa**

BLOODY COMMAS

By **T.J. Edwards**

IF LOVING HIM IS WRONG…

By **Jelissa**

A DISTINGUISHED THUG STOLE MY HEART

By **Meesha**

PUSH IT TO THE LIMIT

By **Bre' Hayes**

BLOOD OF A BOSS **I II & III**

By **Askari**

THE STREETS BLEED MURDER **I, II & III**

THE HEART OF A GANGSTA

By **Jerry Jackson**

CUM FOR ME

CUM FOR ME 2

CUM FOR ME 3

An **LDP Erotica Collaboration**

BRIDE OF A HUSTLA **I & II**

THE FETTI GIRLS **I, II& II**

By **Destiny Skai**

WHEN A GOOD GIRL GOES BAD

By **Adrienne**

A GANGSTER'S REVENGE **I II III & IV**

THE BOSS MAN'S DAUGHTERS

THE BOSS MAN'S DAUGHTERS II

A SAVAGE LOVE **I & II**

BAE BELONGS TO ME

A HUSTLER'S DECEIT I, II

By **Aryanna**

A KINGPIN'S AMBITON

A KINGPIN'S AMBITION **II**

I MURDER FOR THE DOUGH

By **Ambitious**

TRUE SAVAGE

TRUE SAVAGE II

By **Chris Green**

A DOPEBOY'S PRAYER

By **Eddie "Wolf" Lee**

WHAT ABOUT US **I & II**

NEVER LOVE AGAIN

THUG ADDICTION

By **Kim Kaye**

THE KING CARTEL **I, II & III**

By **Frank Gresham**

THESE NIGGAS AIN'T LOYAL **I, II & III**

By **Nikki Tee**

GANGSTA SHYT **I II &III**

By **CATO**

THE ULTIMATE BETRAYAL

By **Phoenix**

BOSS'N UP **I & II**

By **Royal Nicole**

I LOVE YOU TO DEATH

By Destiny J

I RIDE FOR MY HITTA

I STILL RIDE FOR MY HITTA

By **Misty Holt**

LOVE & CHASIN' PAPER

By **Qay Crockett**

TO DIE IN VAIN

By **ASAD**

BOOKS BY LDP'S CEO, CA$H

TRUST IN NO MAN

TRUST IN NO MAN 2

TRUST IN NO MAN 3

BONDED BY BLOOD

SHORTY GOT A THUG

THUGS CRY

THUGS CRY 2

THUGS CRY 3

TRUST NO BITCH

TRUST NO BITCH 2

TRUST NO BITCH 3

TIL MY CASKET DROPS

RESTRAINING ORDER

RESTRAINING ORDER 2

IN LOVE WITH A CONVICT

Coming Soon

BONDED BY BLOOD 2

BOW DOWN TO MY GANGSTA